BENEATH THE SURFACE

HARPER BLISS

Also by Harper Bliss

In the Distance There Is Light
No Strings Attached
The Road to You
Far from the World We Know
Seasons of Love
Release the Stars
Once in a Lifetime
At the Water's Edge
French Kissing: Season Three
French Kissing: Season Two
French Kissing: Season One
High Rise (The Complete Collection)

ISBN-13 978-988-14910-4-6

For the members of my Launch Team. You always perk me up.
Thank you.

1997

CHAPTER ONE

Sheryl checked her watch. She'd told Aimee repeatedly she didn't have time to chat, but Aimee, her boss, never listened. She just talked. And when Aimee talked, Sheryl had to listen. But Sheryl could hardly be holier than thou about running late. It wasn't as if she didn't have a very persistent tendency to be tardy for many appointments, no matter how hard she tried to manage her time properly. But this was not an appointment to be late for. When Sterling Wines agrees to sponsor your fundraising party, you have to show your gratitude by, at the very least, showing up before the delivery guy arrives.

Sheryl rounded the corner and jogged into the alley that held the back entrance to the party venue for the next day. She didn't see anyone waiting for her. She relaxed her pace to a brisk walk and felt for the door key in her pocket. She breathed a sigh of relief: she'd made it on time to accept the generous wine delivery. The other women on the organizing committee would be there soonish to help stock the refrigerators with the about-to-be delivered wine, but Sheryl was in charge of smooth acceptance of the goods. She, Sheryl Johnson, who didn't drink a drop of alcohol, who didn't know the faintest thing about wines and their grapes of origin and what made them palatable, had been in charge of procuring the sponsorship.

Just as she inserted the key into the lock, a white van pulled up at the entrance of the alley. She looked as a man dressed much like herself—jeans and a T-shirt—jumped out, followed by a woman whose pale gray skirt suit didn't exactly indicate she'd come to help unload the boxes.

Sheryl had only spoken to Miss Park on the phone. She had no real reason to be present for a simple wine delivery. Sheryl straightened her posture as the woman walked toward her while the man opened the side door of the van and started unloading boxes onto a trolley.

"Miss Johnson," the woman said, hand extended. "I'm Kristin Park." She gave Sheryl a quick once-over and followed up with a smile that seemed to show a little appreciation for the way Sheryl had clinched a sponsorship deal worth a few hundred dollars—a fortune for the LAUS.

"Very nice to meet you, Miss Park," Sheryl tipped her head and took Kristin's hand in hers. *Very nice indeed.* She let her gaze linger a little longer than was perhaps socially acceptable in a situation like this. Sheryl couldn't in good faith claim her gaydar was alerting her to something, but of course Miss Park knew exactly what kind of event her company was sponsoring.

"We're trying to make inroads with the lesbian community as well as with the gay one," she'd said when Sheryl had first called up the marketing department of Australia's largest wine distributor. *How very advanced of you*, Sheryl had thought, while her eyes rolled all the way to the back of her head. But she knew she had to be grateful because, even though things were slowly shifting—and Mardi Gras was turning into a celebration more than a march for rights every year that passed—not every company would be willing to sponsor this Mardi Gras fundraising party that the university's lesbian association was throwing.

"And you," Miss Park said, "please call me Kristin." Was she responding to Sheryl's glance? To the way she narrowed her eyes and pulled the corner of her mouth into a hint of a smile—not too much so as not to offend?

"How very nice of you to come all the way down here." Sheryl tried a full-on smile now.

"It's no trouble," Kristin said. "Just a good excuse to

get out of the office on a Friday afternoon."

"Would you like to inspect the venue where your wares will be served?" Sheryl gestured at the open door. Meanwhile, the delivery man had piled boxes onto his trolley and was rolling it in their direction.

"Sure." Kristin followed Sheryl inside.

Sheryl flipped on the lights. The venue was small—especially compared to where the boys partied—and Sheryl hoped it would be packed tomorrow. She eyed the room. They had a lot of work to do before then. But Sheryl got that tingling feeling deep inside her belly that it would be good. Excitement mixed with a sense of contributing to her community. The concept of Gay Pride wasn't foreign to her. If anything, it was the only thing she hadn't struggled with throughout her formative years. When everything else was going to hell, Sheryl always had that to hold on to. That and the fact she wasn't born ten years earlier. That she had come of age in the eighties, when LGBT youth groups started popping up in Sydney—an agonizing one-hour bus ride from Campbelltown where she lived with her father, who didn't much care what she was up to, anyway.

Sheryl had found her community early on and it had made her thrive, of that she was sure. Now it was time to give back. Out of gratitude for the people who had come before her and battled for her rights in a way she would never have to, and for everyone who was less fortunate than her. The women's studies department of the University of Sydney where she was doing her PhD was a veritable paradise for lesbians.

"I can see the potential," Kristin said, snapping Sheryl out of her reverie.

Sheryl plastered the most seductive grin on her face she could muster and turned to Kristin. "Your name is on the guest list, of course. You're very welcome to come see for yourself how Sydney's lesbians are enjoying your wine."

Kristin gave a nervous laugh—the first sign of her

being nervous at all. "Maybe I will," she said.

"I'll look out for you." Sheryl had to stop herself from winking.

"Where do you want these?" the delivery man asked.

"Just over there by the bar, please," Sheryl said, and the moment had passed. Though she had a sneaking suspicion Kristin might very well show up tomorrow night. "I'll give you a hand." Sheryl helped unload the boxes from the trolley so the man could go for the next round in the van while, from the corner of her eye, she watched Kristin walk about the venue. She stood where the dance floor would be, and Sheryl tried to picture her dancing under the pulsating light, wondered if she danced at all. Maybe she would find out tomorrow. Maybe.

———

Kristin paced in front of her bedroom mirror. She hadn't planned to go to this party. She hadn't even planned to escort the wine delivery yesterday afternoon. Sterling Wines sponsored many events. If she accompanied every delivery, she wouldn't get any actual work done. But Sheryl Johnson had sent her a leaflet with the Lesbian Association of the University of Sydney's mission statement and a group picture of the women who ran it. She'd read the names underneath the picture with great interest, hoping she'd come across Sheryl, whose deep, warm voice she'd only heard on the phone.

When she reached Sheryl, crouching in the bottom left corner of the picture, she'd found herself uttering a little appreciative sound in the back of her throat. That wide, confident smile. Those light blue eyes. Kristin didn't really know what her type was, although, as she approached thirty, she was quite certain her type was female and not male. The image of Sheryl combined with her voice had convinced her to call up Ari in the warehouse and ask him to wait for her so she could tag along on the delivery for the LAUS.

And now there she stood. Kristin didn't like parties

with loud, thumping music. Places where people were ogled and scored for how they looked. She had plenty of suitable attire for the many work receptions she had to attend, but what on earth did one wear to a lesbian party? And would there only be women? She'd felt a warm rush of something travel through her when Sheryl suggested she come to the party, as though she had somehow known that Kristin was only there that afternoon to meet her in the flesh.

Goodness, she was being silly. She wasn't going to that party. She really didn't have anything to wear. This was not what she did. Which was exactly the reason Kristin hadn't extensively tested her newfound self-awareness—or was it acceptance?—that no man would ever do to her what a woman could.

She'd gone on a couple of dates with women who had advertised in the classifieds' section of *Lesbians on the Loose*. One of them had been quite nice. Maybe not exactly what Kristin was looking for, but really, how could she possibly know what she *was* looking for? She and Petra had gone out a couple of times, had sort of hit it off, and Kristin had—foolishly—believed that was it.

She was sleeping with a woman for the first time in her life, and even though the sky didn't come crashing down, it was infinitely more pleasurable to be touched by a woman's hands than by a man's. Because Kristin didn't know any better, she believed she had found *The One*. Until, only five dates into their short-lived affair, Petra told her it wouldn't work out. Kristin's heart wasn't broken, but the rejection stung enough to have her retreat. She even, if only for a split second, considered going back to men because it would be so much easier. Her parents would be happy, for one. Now they—almost silently—tolerated that Kristin wasn't even engaged to be married on the cusp of her thirtieth birthday.

Kristin looked at herself in the mirror again. She had to go. She could call Cassie and ask her to join. Kristin knew Cassie would do that for her. Apart from the women Kristin had furtively dated, Cassie was her only friend who knew about her wanting to be with women.

"Don't be such a coward," she said to her reflection. "You're not like this. You're not like this at all." Kristin had found that saying things out loud to herself worked toward spurring her into action. It wasn't enough to think it or whisper it. The thought had to be voiced as loud and combative as possible. She conjured up Sheryl's smile. Had she known that Kristin was a lesbian? Kristin didn't think she looked like one at all, though it was starting to dawn on her, perhaps lesbians came in all shapes and sizes. *Ha.* What a novel idea. So what had given her away? The way she carried herself? Just her being there? Or perhaps Sheryl was just guessing. Perhaps she had even been engaging in some wishful thinking?

"I'm going to this party," Kristin said out loud. "I'm a grown woman. Less than two weeks away from turning thirty. I am going to that lesbian party." She took a deep breath, dug out a pair of jeans she didn't often wear and a red blouse from her closet, applied a minimal amount of makeup, and went on her way.

CHAPTER TWO

Sheryl had put herself down for three shifts at the party. The LAUS only had so many volunteers and she wasn't that much of a dancer anyway. If she was working, she could do what she liked to do: look. She'd taken the first shift selling drink tokens, when the queue was still short, but someone had to be there for the early birds. Now she was on admission duty, collecting cover charges and doling out stamps to partygoers. Both jobs gave her an excellent opportunity to scout who turned up. Most of the faces were familiar, but she was pleased to note, many of the women she had never seen before, which meant that whatever PR they had done for this party had reached its target audience.

Inevitably, a few of Aimee's students had showed up, one of whom had been ogling her from a spot across the hallway for at least half an hour. Not all TAs adhered to the university's no fraternizing rule—Sheryl had seen that in action quite a few times since she had started the PhD program—but she wasn't one of *those*. It was unethical. Although, of course, Professor Aimee White herself was notorious for picking a different student to bed each semester.

"Notoriety is not known for it's truthfulness," Aimee had told Sheryl when, in an extremely unguarded moment, Sheryl had confronted her with the rumors.

Sheryl sighed. She would talk to the girl later, after this shift had ended. She'd be cordial but distant enough to make clear that whatever was in the girl's head was never going to happen. Then she focused her attention on the growing queue in front of her. The crowd was gathering. She was surrounded by lesbians and undoubtedly a few straight allies. Before every event, within LAUS, they always had very heated discussions on whether men were allowed in. Sheryl always argued for all-inclusiveness, but not all her colleagues shared her vision. In fact, most of them didn't.

"Hey." Sheryl had been focused on receiving much-needed money for the cause and stamping the inside of people's hands when a familiar voice caught her attention. She looked up and straight into Kristin Park's face. Her lipstick matched her blouse, and oh my, Sheryl liked the non-business look on her—a lot.

"You came." A huge smile spread on Sheryl's lips.

"I did." Kristin offered her hand. Sheryl took it in hers and, as gently as she could, applied the ink of the stamp to the skin of her palm, as though Kristin's hand was much more delicate than all the other hands she had treated to the same ink before, and the application of it needed special care.

"Enjoy the party." She shot Kristin an encouraging smile. "I'll be done here in a bit."

Sheryl didn't have time to watch Kristin be swallowed up by the ever-growing crowd. She had people to admit to the party, and the rest of her shift was spent on automatic pilot, working as fast as she could. Sheryl was no stranger to organizing parties like this. She'd joined LAUS as a student almost ten years ago, when it had still been in its infancy and they had trouble being recognized as an official university association. She was a veteran now. It took bigger things to faze her than a long queue of women eager to party. Like the thought of Kristin on the dance floor, being hit on by someone else. Sheryl couldn't wait for her shift to end. Kristin had come, which could only mean one thing.

———

As Kristin advanced into the mass of women—more women than she'd ever seen gathered in one place—she hoped she wouldn't run into Petra. Or anyone from work—though would that really be so bad? After picking up some drink tokens, she made her way to the bar and ordered a glass of white wine. She was glad to find it nicely chilled and welcomed that first fresh sip sliding down her throat. A few more of those and most of her nerves would be kept at bay.

She tried to catch a glimpse of Sheryl, but there were too many people between her and the entrance. She checked her watch and hoped that Sheryl's shift would end on the hour. Though she shouldn't get her hopes up too high. Kristin was sure a woman like Sheryl had plenty of admirers. Perhaps she even had a girlfriend and she'd just been courteous to Kristin yesterday afternoon. Even so, no matter the status of Sheryl's love life, Kristin applauded herself for making it there. Not only had she taken a big step, she was supporting a good cause, which was as much her own as all the other women present.

Granted, the music was a little loud, smoke hung thick in the air, and she was forced to stand a little too close to strangers for her comfort, but she was there, and that's what mattered. She had come on her own. She was no longer a coward hiding behind the myriad of work-related events she could always choose to attend on any given weekend night. Networking never stopped, and it was the perfect excuse for someone like Kristin to neglect her personal needs. She was career-oriented, she always told herself. Work came first. It was easy enough to win that argument with herself.

Kristin downed her wine and elbowed her way through the crowd at the bar to fetch another. A woman with a long blond braid hung over her shoulder smiled at her and Kristin smiled back. She actually knew the song the DJ had just put on, and her hips, as if of their own accord, started to swing a little. This was a lot more fun than another restaurant opening or the re-opening of a bar where she was always hit on by men she wasn't remotely interested in but had to give a little bit of her attention to nonetheless because why else was she there but to network?

At this party, she could be the part of her she'd kept hidden for too long. The side of her her family must know about, though talking about it would be considered a grave faux pas. Don't ask, don't tell all the way. The thought of just being herself at this party was so freeing, so exhilarating, she didn't mind any longer when someone bumped her shoulder into hers or spilled some beer on her shoes. A tingle ignited in her belly at the sight of the two women on the outskirts of the dance floor, kissing with no qualms. The whole atmosphere of the place was intoxicating.

"Hey, stranger." Then, seemingly out of nowhere, Sheryl stood next to her. "Are you having fun?" She eyed Kristin's drink. "I hope you didn't pay to drink your own wine."

Kristin chuckled. "It's not *my* wine, it's my company's. And yes, I'm having fun."

"Good." Sheryl shuffled her weight from one foot to the other while her gaze was fixed on Kristin. "Truth be told, I wasn't expecting you."

It was night-club dark around them, but Kristin could still clearly see the blue of Sheryl's eyes. "Yet here I am," she said in what she hoped was a flirtatious tone.

"Well, you were on the guest list so…"

"An opportunity not to be missed." Kristin knocked back the last of her wine.

"How about I get you another one of those?" Sheryl pointed at Kristin's empty glass.

Just then, the DJ decided to change tack and the first, slow notes of "Show Me Heaven" started playing.

"How about a dance instead?" Kristin could barely believe she'd just asked another woman to dance. Part of that could be credited to downing two glasses of wine in short order, but not all. Perhaps she just really wanted to dance with Sheryl.

"I can't say no to that after you gave us all that wine."

"I wouldn't want you to feel obligated because you think you owe me," Kristin said, a smile in her voice. "I can assure you it won't affect future sponsorship deals if you decline." This was so much more fun than having to endure aimless flirtations from men at receptions.

"Come on." Sheryl grabbed her hand and Kristin quickly deposited her empty glass on a table on their way to the dance floor, which was already packed with women pressed closely together.

The touch of Sheryl's hand against hers—so different from that handshake the day before—made her break out into a mild sweat. Or perhaps it was the proximity of all those female bodies swaying to the slow beat.

"I love this song," Kristin said, as Sheryl planted her hands on her hips. Instinctively, Kristin put hers on Sheryl's shoulders. They were about the same height and although there was a fair amount of space left between their bodies, the immediate intimacy of dancing together threw Kristin a little.

Sheryl nodded. "I remember going to see the movie, back in the day when I was young and gullible, expecting greatness from Nicole Kidman, our Ozzie pride and joy." She swung Kristin around, and when their bodies realigned, Sheryl's hips were most definitely pushing against Kristin's. Kristin looked into Sheryl's eyes, thoroughly enjoying the press of her hips against hers. She didn't want to ruin the moment by continuing a conversation about Australian actresses conquering Hollywood, or by saying anything at all. Sheryl's hands rode up a little, planting themselves firmly on Kristin's waist. Their faces were so close. Kristin shut her eyes and lost herself in the music and the moment for a few seconds. And to think she almost hadn't come.

They danced in silence until the end of the song. Then their bodies fell apart awkwardly, but Kristin thought it a bit much to ask for the next dance as well.

"How about that drink?" Sheryl asked.

"Oh yes." Kristin needed it.

"I'll be right back." Sheryl headed to the bar.

Kristin watched her until she was out of her line of sight, then looked at the writhing bodies on the dance floor. It was another slow one, but Kristin didn't know the song. The sight of all these women dancing together emboldened her. Sure, she wanted to dance more with Sheryl, but she would also like to have a conversation with her in a more quiet setting.

"None of Sterling Wines' delicious offerings for you?" Kristin looked at the glass of water in Sheryl's hand.

"I'm not much of a drinker." Sheryl shot her a wide smile.

"Oh." Kristin mirrored Sheryl's smile. "And I was just going to ask you to go for a drink with me one of these days."

"How about coffee tomorrow afternoon instead?" Sheryl countered, not missing a beat.

"That sounds like the perfect compromise." Kristin stood there beaming, feeling a little foolish but also very pleased with herself for coming to this party. Who would have thought that her job as junior marketing manager at a wine distribution company would have led to a date with a gorgeous lesbian?

CHAPTER THREE

The biggest advantage of not drinking was the absence of hangovers. Having abstained for most of her adult life, Sheryl had never actually been on the receiving end of a vicious hangover. She had seen them in action often enough, however, when the time came to clean up after a party. Her fellow organizers complained their way through their—often poor—performance of their various tasks. Which was why Sheryl thought it important to be present when the LAUS members removed all evidence of the previous night's party.

Today, she had an even bigger spring in her step than most, because she had a date that very afternoon. A date with Kristin Park, the *wine woman*, as some of her friends referred to her.

"Good job, sister," Caitlin said. "You worked your butt off once again."

"It's not work when it's fun."

"Speaking of fun… I saw you having quite a bit of that with a slender Asian lady last night. Do spill," Caitlin said as they stood leaning against the now-empty bar.

"Yes, Sher, spill." Betty, who had been sweeping the floor, joined them.

"There's nothing to spill just yet, ladies. I am, however, having coffee with her in about three hours."

"Three hours?" Caitlin said. "Then what are you still doing here? Go home, rest up, make sure you look your best for the wine woman."

"What's wrong with how I look now?"

Betty came to stand in front of her, leaning on her

broom. "Let's just say the whole of you could do with some ironing, not just your clothes."

"Thank you very much for injecting me with an extra dose of confidence."

"Confidence is not the issue here," Caitlin butted in. "You already have plenty of that." Two years ago, Sheryl and Caitlin had briefly dated—an affair that had ended in friendship rather than anything long-term.

"Just go, Sheryl. You've more than done your part. We'll make sure everything is spic-and-span before we return the key tomorrow," Betty said. "Trust your sisters." She shot Sheryl a goofy wink. "Go, go, go. And we'll be wanting all the juicy details at the meeting on Tuesday."

———

They had agreed to meet at a coffee shop not far from the university, just because Sheryl knew the opening hours by heart—and perhaps also because it was halfway between her apartment and her work place. But despite living nearer their rendezvous place, Sheryl was last to arrive. How did that happen? She had been constantly checking her watch to make sure to leave on time.

Kristin seemed totally absorbed by the book she was reading and didn't look up when Sheryl entered the establishment. This gave Sheryl a chance to have a good look at Kristin before they actually started the date. Her appearance was pretty immaculate for someone who had knocked back the wine so easily and into the small hours last night. Her short hair looked like it was styled by a professional. She sat straight-backed, her attention to what she was reading unwavering. Sheryl made a mental note to find out which book it was and add it to her never-ending to-read pile.

"That seems mighty interesting," Sheryl said.

Kristin looked up, a smile appearing on her face instantly. "Hey." Her voice was soft, and when she looked up like that, Sheryl could make out some signs of fatigue around her eyes. The telltale frown of the forehead. Sheryl might not have had any hangovers in her life herself, but she'd had ample opportunity to study the effects of them up close. Kristin rose and promptly grabbed Sheryl by the shoulders before pressing a quick kiss to her cheek.

"What are you reading?" Sheryl hoped to mask the blush she felt creep up her neck with her question.

"The latest Kay Scarpetta," Kristin said. "Are you a Patricia Cornwell fan?"

They both sat down, even though Sheryl hadn't ordered her coffee yet. "I wish I had the time to read for leisure, but that's not a luxury I have right now."

"So what do you do for leisure, I wonder."

"I'll tell you all the fascinating details about my life after I get us a much-needed cup of coffee." On her way to the counter, Sheryl weighed Kristin's choice of reading material. There had been a time in her life when she'd been terribly snobbish about such things, and probably wouldn't even have considered dating someone who couldn't quote from *The Female Eunuch* by heart, but she'd long since let go of the lofty aspirations of only dating within the university pool. Besides, perhaps Kristin was well-versed in Germaine Greer.

"So?" Kristin asked after Sheryl had provided them both with steaming beverages. "I'm all curious now. What do you do in your spare time?"

"You saw that in action last night and before that, when I was pestering you to sponsor our party."

"I would hardly call that pestering." A small smile played on Kristin's lips. "Besides, if it hadn't been for the *pestering*, we wouldn't be sitting here right now."

"I did think it kind of strange that someone with the word *manager* in their job title would show up for a wine delivery. You must explain that to me." And just like that, the entire atmosphere surrounding them turned flirty again. They'd only just met, but it seemed like their go-to mode. There was something in the air when they were in each other's company. It couldn't be denied. It also kept a wide grin glued to Sheryl's face throughout the conversation.

"So it's all work for you all the time?" Kristin asked, letting her gaze pass over Sheryl once again. How was it even possible for someone to look so scrumptious in so simple an outfit? Jeans and a t-shirt was all it took for Sheryl.

"Not really, but I do spend most of my time at the university and it is all a bit intertwined, but grading a paper is hardly the same as throwing a party." There was something about Sheryl that had instantly spoken to Kristin. It had even come through in her voice when they'd only talked on the phone. A certain gravitas beyond her years. And then when they'd met in person, a tiny glimmer of melancholy in her glance that made her look older and as though she took even the smallest matter very seriously.

While Kristin considered herself lighthearted enough, she had not had a lighthearted, breezy upbringing. Everything was always dead serious at the Park house, from homework to the automatic assumption that Kristin would follow in both her parents' footsteps and become a doctor—and, of course, that she would meet a fellow doctor-in-training in medical school and marry him, just like her parents had done. While Kristin had defied her parents in most ways, part of the seriousness had stuck.

When it was time for a refill, it was Kristin's turn to head to the counter and as she walked back, mugs in hand, she considered that she could sit here in this coffee shop in Sheryl's exquisite company for a good while longer.

"What about your work?" Sheryl asked. "How many Mardi Gras fundraising parties do you sponsor? This must be a busy time for you."

"We do have standards, and we are quite selective about who we give our wares to." Kristin remembered, as though it had only happened yesterday, the call that had been dispatched through to her—as most calls related to marketing that reception didn't know what to do with were —and the deep voice on the other end of the line. Without the visual, someone else might have mistaken Sheryl's low voice for a man's, but she hadn't.

"I feel honored then." Sheryl cocked her head. "Do you enjoy what you do?"

Kristin nodded. "Very much so. I feel like I'm exactly where I need to be. I had a later start than most of my colleagues because of a failed med school experiment." For reasons Kristin didn't fully understand, the marketing department at Sterling Wines was mostly populated by women. Women who were her peers age-wise, but were now all, as though collectively struck by the notion of the biological clock, starting to have families. No matter how women-unfriendly the conclusion—though really, it was more a reflection on how corporations, at the top, were still too male dominated—Kristin knew this gave her an edge over her colleagues.

"A marketing late bloomer, huh?"

"I know that marketing seems like this catch-all for students who don't really know what to do with their lives or, like me, realized, two years in, that practicing medicine would make them miserable, but for me, it was never like that."

"So why the two-year detour?"

Kristin couldn't help but roll her eyes. "A case of parental pressure and expectations. I'm an only child, so my parents piled all their big hopes onto me."

"And they wanted you to be a doctor."

"I know it's a big cliché, what with me being Korean and my Korean immigrant parents, both doctors, wanting me to become a doctor. I guess it's a cliché for a reason."

"Good for you for standing up to them."

Kristin chuckled. "When I dropped out of med school, my mother suggested I become a nurse instead." She shook her head. "I always had other dreams for myself, but perhaps

I was just slow in realizing it. First, I thought my aversion to all things medical stemmed from being the daughter of two doctors. That I would get over it if I just plunged in headfirst. When that didn't happen after the first year, I figured I owed it to them to at least meet one of their expectations because I guess, somehow, I already knew I wouldn't be meeting another big one."

"Ah." Sheryl's eyes narrowed. She listened with such attention visible on her face. She sat with one leg slung over the other, looking at Kristin as if learning all about her was the most important thing in life. Maybe to her, in this moment, it was. The thought made Kristin go all warm inside. "*That.*"

"I'll be thirty in three days and I'm not out to my parents. I'm not out pretty much anywhere, really."

"You'll get there when the time is right."

Kristin quirked up her eyebrows.

"What?" Sheryl asked.

"I don't know. I guess I would have expected a more militant reaction from you." She followed up with a grin.

"Just like you are not a cliché, but a complex human being with reasons for why things happened the way they did in your life, neither am I."

"You will make an excellent professor one day, Sheryl Johnson."

Sheryl laughed a deep belly laugh. "That's the plan. If I can ever finish my bloody thesis."

In the short moment of silence that followed, Kristin felt all the things she'd never felt with Petra. All the things that, deep down, she knew she was capable of feeling but hadn't had the occasion to.

———

"I think they want us to leave," Sheryl said. They were the only patrons left, and had both switched to tea after the third cup of coffee.

"Pity." Kristin looked around. "I like this place. I have a

bit of a coffee shop fetish in general and this place ticks all my boxes."

"Maybe I'll see you here again some day then." Sheryl leaned forward, elbows on knees.

Kristin mirrored her image. "There's a really good chance of that."

"How about tomorrow, whenever it is you knock off work?"

"Or…" Kristin didn't want to go home to her empty flat. She didn't want to sit on her sofa and wait for tomorrow to come around, regretting not having said what she was about to say. "We could go for dinner now? Are you hungry?"

Sheryl sucked her bottom lip into her mouth and nodded her head slowly. "That sounds very enticing."

"But?"

"No buts. I know just the place." Sheryl rose and led the way.

The relief that washed over Kristin was comparable to what she'd felt when she finally did make the decision to quit medical school. It wasn't only relief coursing through her, however, but the burgeoning sense that her life was about to change for the better. Just like it had done before.

CHAPTER FOUR

"You don't drink at all?" Kristin asked.

Sheryl considered herself lucky that the question had only come by the time they were halfway through the meal. Usually she was bombarded by quizzical looks and inordinate questions when wine was to be ordered—because God forbid someone in Australia had dinner without alcohol just once in their lives. For all its virtues and relaxed vibes, this country was obsessed with becoming intoxicated on any given night after five. Sheryl knew this was a *slight* exaggeration, but she couldn't help but be fanatical about it. And nobody in their right mind could deny that Australians in general liked a drink—or five.

"I do. I just don't like what it does to my brain. I like to be clear-headed. Life is short, why waste it on being out of it? I'd much rather be in it, you know?" Sheryl laughed at herself—she was good at that in situations like this. "I'm gibbering." She was on a date with a beautiful woman. She wasn't about to reveal the real reason for her abstinence. If this worked out, they would have plenty of time to discuss that.

"That doesn't sound like gibberish to me at all."

"And that from someone who works in the wine industry."

"I don't really see myself as working in the wine industry per se. I work in marketing."

"Fair enough." Sheryl deposited her cutlery on her plate.

"So what about *your* parents?" Kristin asked, kind of

23

out of the blue. In the context of a date, and in light of what Kristin had told Sheryl about her own parents already, it was a logical question, but Sheryl wondered at the timing of it. Or maybe Kristin had a strongly developed sense of female intuition.

"My mother died a long time ago and my father and I are not close." Sheryl didn't say anything more, but it was always interesting to see how people reacted to a conversation-stopper like that.

"I'm sorry to hear that," Kristin said. She genuinely looked sorry, too. As long as she didn't pity Sheryl. Or ask any follow-up questions. Ironically, it was when questions like these came up, that Sheryl hankered for the unknown effects of a drink the most. "That must not have been easy."

If anything, Kristin displayed great empathy, and frankly, the woman was so gorgeous, so kind, so easy to be around, that Sheryl wouldn't hold any reaction against her.

"Do I look like someone who has led a hard-knock life?" Sheryl leaned back and opened her arms.

Kristin laughed. "You look beautiful." Her voice had gone earnest.

Sheryl responded in kind. "So do you." That short black hair. Those dark, expressive eyes. The warm color of her skin. Sheryl remembered last night's dance. She had wanted to pull Kristin a whole lot closer than she actually had, but didn't think it appropriate for a first dance—a first real contact.

Kristin's smile grew wider. "Is this where we cross over into the super mushy part of the date?"

"Either that or we have dessert," Sheryl said, deflating some of the tension that had mounted.

"I do love a nice piece of pavlova." Kristin narrowed her eyes to slits at the last word, and Sheryl couldn't help but feel that Kristin was not talking about a fruit-topped meringue.

———

Kristin was exhausted but elated as they stood outside the restaurant. Summer was in full swing, but mid-December evenings in Sydney were usually cooler and pleasant.

"What's next?" she asked.

"I guess that depends," Sheryl said. "How early do your marketing duties start tomorrow morning?"

"No matter what happens tonight, work will start too early tomorrow, so that's really not a factor." Kristin had ended up having only one glass of wine with dinner—out of a strange sense of solidarity with Sheryl and her non-drinking habits—but it seemed to have gone straight to her head. Or maybe it was something else causing the headiness in her brain, the lightness in her feet despite the fatigue, and the will for this evening to never end, no matter how early she had to get up in the morning.

"I live just two blocks away. I don't have much to offer in the way of nightcaps and I'd venture a guess that we've had enough coffee and tea for one day, but I do have a lovely bottle of mineral water itching to be opened," Sheryl said.

"Now there's an offer I can't refuse." Kristin already loved the way Sheryl used ten words when two would suffice. The intensity in her eyes when she explained something. Even the way she held back when it came to certain, too personal, topics. Kristin was not raised to overshare, nor to be overly emotional. She recognized a certain stoicism in Sheryl that she could appreciate. A restraint that she, too, craved. Though, as they walked to Sheryl's building, she hoped all restraint would be loosened when it came to their first kiss. She already wanted it so badly, had found herself staring at Sheryl's mouth as she spoke—even as she ate—with growing impatience, wondering what these lips would feel like on hers, and somehow knowing they would be impossibly soft and so, so right.

Every time she was preparing for a date with Petra, Kristin had been hopeful and had tried to convince herself that she'd finally found what she was looking for. But every passionless date had confirmed a little more that it was not enough. And now, walking through the falling night with Sheryl, she knew for certain she'd been right. *This* was how it was supposed to feel, this was *it*.

When they rounded a corner, and bumped into each other inadvertently, Sheryl took the opportunity to grab for Kristin's hand and held it in hers for the rest of the walk. As their steps echoed on the sidewalk, Kristin felt the realization flare somewhere deep inside of her that she wasn't just walking in the direction of Sheryl's apartment, but toward something a lot bigger than that.

"I'm afraid grad students don't live like queens," Sheryl said.

Kristin let her glance wander around the place. It was small but tidy enough—perhaps some impromptu cleaning up had happened before Sheryl left that afternoon? Her own apartment wasn't much better. Only six months ago, with her thirtieth birthday looming, Kristin had moved out of an apartment she shared with two other women, one a colleague, the other the colleague's friend. She'd traded in space for privacy and what she'd thought of as a necessary level of independence for the start of her fourth decade.

"Nor do junior marketing managers, let me assure you," Kristin said. While Sheryl busied herself in the kitchenette, Kristin walked to a bookshelf that took up almost an entire wall. She found a lot of text books and, in the far right upper corner, almost out of sight, a picture of a woman with whom Sheryl shared some distinct features. Well, mainly the blue of her eyes and that little pout in her lips when she smiled. Kristin thought it wise to not ask any questions about Sheryl's deceased mother. She didn't see any pictures of someone who could be Sheryl's father, nor any family snaps—the kind that were featured everywhere in Kristin's own apartment.

"Here you go." Sheryl handed Kristin a glass of water.

"Shall we sit?"

"Nice place," Kristin said, and meant it. Her own apartment, close to the CBD so she could walk to work, was about the same size, much more modern, but a lot less cozy.

"It's not much, but it's convenient. And you might not believe it, but more than twenty people have been in here. At the same time."

"I guess I can imagine it if I tilt my head this way and try not to think about what kind of party it was you were throwing."

Sheryl huffed out a chuckle. "One with a lot of shouting and posturing. LAUS meetings can get a bit... overheated at times."

"I bet you slept well that night."

Sheryl rolled her eyes. "I adore women who have a strong sense of self and firm opinions, but twenty of them crammed in the same room is a bit much, even for me."

"Poor you," Kristin joked. "All those women."

Sheryl put her glass of water on the table. "One is just enough for me." She bit into her bottom lip again, the way Kristin had seen her do a couple of times already.

Kristin racked her brain to come up with a witty reply, but nothing materialized. So she sat there, Sheryl's comment hanging in the air, looking into those blue, blue eyes. They were the kind of blue she'd witnessed being photoshopped onto a model whose eyes weren't deemed blue enough to sell a particular brand of wine. At the time, Kristin had greatly questioned whether a lighter hue of blue mattered, but now, staring into the real deal, she could see that it did. How it made all the difference.

Sheryl shuffled a little closer to Kristin on the couch. She had drawn up a knee, which now bumped lightly into Kristin's side, startling her out of her reverie on shades of blue.

"Your eyes," she stammered.

"Have the most beautiful view at this very moment,"

Sheryl added. Oh, how suave she was. Sheryl angled her head and leaned in. She paused, blinked, and softly pressed her lips to Kristin's.

Kristin was still holding her glass of water. She wanted to just let it fall to the floor and wrap her arms around Sheryl's neck, the way she had done when they were dancing last night, but with so much more intention behind it. Instead, after the first soft peck. Kristin hurriedly disposed of it, not letting her gaze leave Sheryl's exquisite face for one split second.

The next time their lips met, the air in the room had already changed, had already gone from the possibility of kissing to wondering where it would end. But Kristin did her best not to think of that, and focused on the moment—on the here and now instead of the near and distant future, unlike what she'd been told to do so many times when she was younger—and to let her senses fully enjoy the fact that she was kissing another woman. For a lesbian—because, yes, she was exactly that—on the cusp of thirty, she hadn't done a lot of that yet. Not nearly enough.

As Sheryl's tongue probed her lips, Kristin couldn't help but wonder how many lips that tongue had ventured past. Sheryl looked like a woman of experience—she'd even sounded like one on the phone. That was one of the reasons Kristin had felt so instantly attracted to her. She longed for someone like Sheryl; someone to show her what it was all about. This lesbian life she so hankered for but had, somehow, missed. She had so many questions to ask Sheryl, so much of her presumed knowledge to feast on. But right then, they were kissing, and Kristin's neglected body was starting to react.

When they paused, Kristin tried to anchor herself into the moment again, even though she had no idea how. Her mind was racing, thinking all these thoughts that should just be erased by the touch of another woman's lips on hers. She looked at Sheryl, at her hair that fell loosely to her shoulders

—perhaps the most overtly feminine aspect of her. At those eyes that said so much, of that Kristin was certain, but she had no means to decipher their language. This was already so much more than anything she'd ever felt. The intensity of this kiss made her feel as though she'd previously only dabbled in lesbianism, dipped her toe into the proverbial waters just a fraction, whereas now her entire body appeared to be sucked under.

Kristin pulled back slightly and realized she was reacting in her usual way to her body's growing excitement. It was as if she was conditioned to mitigate her visible enthusiasm, to put a lid on that scandalous sensation.

"Are you all right?" Sheryl asked, her voice husky and sweet.

"I am," Kristin said, and leaned in. She kissed Sheryl now, or at least instigated the next kiss. Because she was more all right than she'd ever been, optimistic and so very certain of one thing: she wanted Sheryl's lips on hers over and over again.

———

Sheryl caught her breath. Kristin was giving some mixed signals. She was harder to read than most women. There was something guarded about her, a wall that would probably only be broken down piece by tiny piece. She'd noticed that when they first shook hands at the wine delivery. Everything about that half hour they'd spent in each other's company— that very first time they'd clasped eyes on each other—had been a mixed signal. But a signal nonetheless. A challenge Sheryl was more than up for.

Should she go for that top button of Kristin's blouse or would that be construed as too forward? This was a perfect example of how Kristin made Sheryl doubt her otherwise instinctive actions. Sheryl was not the type to debate herself on whether she should start unbuttoning another woman's blouse. She had undressed quite a few women so far and none of them had ever complained. Sheryl always followed her gut, and doing so had never let her down. So what was with all the back and forth now? Maybe she was just projecting her own insecurities because, damn it, she really liked Kristin. She didn't want to mess this up. This could be the start of something Sheryl had been waiting for a long time.

Sheryl let her hand slip from Kristin's neck to where her blouse gaped open at her collarbone. She traced a finger over Kristin's skin there. Ha, she didn't even have to unbutton that top button. She already had plenty of access to Kristin's skin. Oh, Kristin's skin. That pert mouth. God, this woman sitting on her couch, kissing her, was stunning. Everything about her was delicate in a way that seemed opposite to Sheryl. Even this blouse she was wearing. It made Sheryl's simple T-shirt feel like a cliché.

That's when it hit her. Kristin made Sheryl shake in her boots—made her feel so unlike herself—because she was already infatuated with her. Caitlin would mock her for even considering the possibility after only an extended evening in someone's company. Betty would encourage her. But what would Sheryl say if anyone else told her about her current situation? And what the hell was she doing asking herself a question like that? Yes, Kristin unsettled her, but in a good way. In the most exquisite way possible.

This was the beginning of something that Sheryl never wanted to end, which was why she wouldn't be unbuttoning any blouses tonight. This moment had to be approached with restraint and respect.

"What are you doing next weekend?" Sheryl asked when they broke next from their lip-lock.

Kristin pulled her lips into an O. "I think there's a strong possibility that next weekend I'll be doing whatever you're about to suggest next."

"Good." Sheryl nodded. "I'd like to take you somewhere."

"Oh yeah? Where to?"

"It's a surprise."

Kristin cocked her head. "I barely know you, Sheryl. How can I let you take me *somewhere* if I don't know where it is?"

"I dare say you know me well enough already." Sheryl pulled Kristin closer again, kissed her again.

CHAPTER FIVE

Kristin hadn't stopped thinking about Sheryl all week. Work weeks usually flew by, never leaving Kristin enough time to finish her daily to-do lists. More often than not, she found herself popping into the office on Saturday morning to finish her tasks and have a clean-ish slate to return to the next Monday. This week, however, had gone by at an excruciatingly slow pace.

A few months prior, Kristin had received a portable phone courtesy of Sterling Wines—just another instrument to keep her busy when she wasn't in the office—but apparently PhD students at the University of Sydney did not receive the same benefits. This meant that Kristin couldn't call Sheryl in the evening because the woman was always busy at some meeting.

Sheryl's only free night that week had been Monday, and that was the night Kristin was hosting an event at a new wine bar in Pott's Point. Sheryl wasn't only writing her thesis on the evolution of the butch identity in modern queer culture. She was also an essential member of the Lesbian Association of the University of Sydney, of the Sydney Mardi Gras organizing committee, and it seemed to Kristin, a whole host of other lesbian-related organizations. Sheryl lived and breathed lesbianism and feminism, and it kept her very busy.

They managed a quick lunch together on Wednesday—oddly, Sheryl seemed to have a lot more free time during the day than in the evenings—which had been a giddy affair of staring into each other's eyes, not consuming a lot of food, and Sheryl teasing Kristin about where she would take her on Saturday, and giving instructions on what to take. Staying overnight was a possibility, if Kristin was up to it.

By the time Friday evening came round, and Kristin met up with Cassie for a much-needed drinking-and-sharing session, Kristin felt that a month had passed instead of a week since she had kissed Sheryl good-bye at the front door of her apartment.

"I've met someone," Kristin blurted out. They had barely sat down at their usual table at The Barrel for their weekly Friday-after-work piss-up. "Her name's Sheryl. We had coffee and dinner on Sunday, and then lunch this week. And she's taking me away somewhere tomorrow, although she hasn't told me where." The words exploded out of her, just like the emotions had been exploding within her all week. Was this love at first sight or something silly like that? Was it the fact that Kristin had not acted upon her desires as much as she would have liked in her twenties? Or maybe it was the relief that when she turned thirty next week, she would be able to look back on the past decade with more than just regrets for what she'd been too afraid to do. As if Sheryl showing up in extremis had made the past ten years worthwhile.

"You're seeing someone," Cassie shouted. "I can't believe it."

"Well, I wouldn't exactly call it *seeing*," Kristin backpedaled a bit. "We've only just met."

"Good grief, Kris," Cassie continued, ignoring Kristin altogether, "that is such a relief."

"Why thank you."

"Don't take this the wrong way, but, at times, I thought you were headed for surefire spinsterhood."

"How can I possibly not take that the wrong way?"

Cassie gently put her hand on Kristin's shoulder. "Because I don't mean it in a bad way. Just in a worried-about-you way. You're a gorgeous person, Krissie, but sometimes it just seems as though you're very reluctant to be happy."

"That's not—" Kristin started to object.

Cassie held up her hand. "I'm not finished and it's very important I finish this thought, okay? I'm your best friend and you only came out to me, what? A year and a half? Two years ago? And you haven't told anyone else since."

"I haven't had that much to tell."

"But what I'm really trying to say is that it doesn't matter how long it took. It's Friday evening, I can tell you're tired, but I can tell there's something else going on as well. Hand on my heart, I can tell just by looking at you, and that makes me so very happy. That's all."

Kristin had no objections. If Cassie had made a similar comment about her future as a spinster just the week before, she would have debated, defended herself, because she was so much more than perpetually single. She had achieved a lot, not in the least professionally—if her boss Nigel was to be believed, a promotion wasn't far off.

"It's early days still," was all Kristin said, after which she allowed herself a minute of the hormonal reverie she'd spent most of the week being lost in. When she was a teenager, and her friends went on and on about this boy or that, Kristin found it so hard to relate. To the point that she started to wonder what on earth was wrong with her. She got it now. She was twenty-nine and she got it.

———

Of all people's, Sheryl had managed to snag Aimee's car for the weekend.

"It's all yours," Aimee had said, dangling the keys in front of her. "Take your girlfriend into the woods with my old Porsche."

The university department where Sheryl spent her days was a hotbed of gossip and being all up in each other's business. Perhaps it was the sort of subjects they studied, or the way their analytical minds were always busy looking for more meaning, more of everything. Their everyday lives were not exempt from the same level of scrutiny. Their work relations depended on having everything out in the open at all times, it was at the very core of what they did, because if it wasn't, what they studied lost a lot of its meaning.

Sheryl didn't own a car herself, she got by on public transport, as did most of her friends, and didn't like how unsure she was behind the wheel. Thank goodness it was early on Saturday morning, and there wasn't that much traffic to negotiate. She was grateful for the short drive to Kristin's place so she could get her bearings in the car, tap into an air of confidence she mostly had to fake because she didn't possess it naturally when she was in the driver's seat.

She waited for Kristin in front of her building, leaning against the hood of the car, her mouth curling into a smile as soon as Kristin exited the front door.

"Wow." Kristin quirked up her eyebrows. "Is that the surprise?"

Sheryl shook her head, drew Kristin near, and kissed her full on the mouth—how was that for following her gut instinct?

Once inside the car, Kristin let her gaze roam around. "I just thought you were more of a VW van kind of girl, you know?"

"I'm not any car kind of girl, as a matter of fact. This is my boss's car, so please treat it with the respect it deserves."

"You should have said. We could have taken mine." Kristin sat there beaming for some reason.

"Then I wouldn't have been able to drive you." This morning, Sheryl was operating fully on instinct, and she put a hand on Kristin's thigh. She was wearing a pair of light linen trousers and Sheryl felt the warmth of her skin come through.

Kristin put her hand on Sheryl's, and they drove in silence for a while. A silence for which Sheryl was grateful so she could focus on the road and get them out of the city and onto the highway. Once they got there, she would be more relaxed—able to rely on gut instinct even more. This whole trip was an exercise in following her intuition. The place she was taking Kristin, though on the surface not that special, held a lot of meaning for Sheryl. And for some reason, she had, out of the blue, invited Kristin there.

———

The cabin was a two-hour drive out of Sydney. Two hours during which Sheryl had luxuriated in Kristin's proximity and, the more distance she put between them and the city, the surer she grew that this had been an excellent idea. She'd never taken a woman on a road trip for a second date—or third date if their quick lunch of Wednesday was to be counted. Although to Sheryl that lunch felt more like an intermezzo, a quick check-in to see if what they'd felt initially the previous weekend was still there. It had become clear very swiftly that it was, the way they'd sat giggling like schoolgirls, ignoring their food and staring into each other's eyes.

"It could be a whirlwind romance," Caitlin had said. "One of those when-you-know-you-know affairs."

"We're almost there." Sheryl turned into a small private lane not very suited for Aimee's Porsche, so they hobbled in their seats for a few minutes, until there it loomed. The cabin Sheryl's grandfather had built. It now belonged to her Aunt Rita, who never came here. As far as she knew, Sheryl was the only one in her family who made use of the cabin. Most people preferred more luxury than what this particular means of accommodation offered, whereas for Sheryl, the real luxury lay in the solitude of the place.

She'd written the best parts of her master's thesis in this cabin, longhand, papers strewn all around her in an organized chaos only she knew the order to. She would come back to do the same when it was crunch time for the dissertation she was currently working on. But this day was no day to think about her thesis—though it was always hard to not have an inkling of it rummaging around in the back of her mind. This day was all about Kristin. Perhaps it was a bold move to bring Kristin here, but it matched Sheryl's bold feelings for her entirely.

"Wow." As soon as the car had come to a standstill, Kristin jumped out. She stood looking at the cabin, hands on her waist, then swiveled her head to take in the surroundings, which were the real draw of the place. Rolling green hills giving way to the mountains that loomed ahead. The sound of a nearby creek, soothing to ears that were used to relentless city noise.

Kristin turned around and looked at Sheryl. "Now I'd better hope I judged you right. What with you dragging me to a remote place like this and nobody knowing where I am."

"Maybe that cellular phone of yours has reception," Sheryl said.

"I hope it doesn't." Kristin took a step closer to Sheryl and reached for her hands. "And you said staying the night was optional?"

"I guess I was trying to not have you pack a pair of pajamas." She slanted her head and kissed Kristin on the cheek.

"Well played." Kristin's voice had already been reduced to a whisper. They hadn't even made it inside the cabin yet, and already Sheryl wanted to tear her clothes off—and finish what she had almost started last Sunday.

"I'd best empty the trunk," Sheryl said when they broke from their kiss. "Wouldn't want the milk to go off."

CHAPTER SIX

Kristin sat on the cabin's porch, overlooking the mountain, with a glass of rather excellent red wine that Sheryl had brought especially for her. Sheryl busied herself with preparing dinner. Kristin had offered to help, but Sheryl had shooed her out of what passed for the kitchen, but was basically one electrical hob and a microwave oven that looked like it could have been one of the first ones ever made.

Last Saturday, around this time, she'd been agonizing over whether to go to the LAUS party or not, and now there she sat, surrounded by the sounds of nature as dusk gathered. She heard Sheryl clatter dishes behind the screen door. The cabin was basic, but Kristin was being pampered nonetheless.

And then there was the tension in the air that had been growing at a steady pace since they'd arrived. Well, since Kristin had slid into the passenger seat of Sheryl's borrowed car, actually. They'd kissed, groped a little, hands venturing farther at each turn, and it was all very exciting, adding to the headiness that started to take over Kristin's mind. This was all so dream-like, so perfect as a beginning, she could hardly imagine it not ever having a happy ending.

Sheryl planted a plate of cold cuts and various cheeses on the tiny outside table, and refilled Kristin's glass of wine gallantly. Despite the cooling atmosphere as evening fell, Kristin could feel a warmth seep into her core brought on by the care Sheryl was showing her.

"You could have at least allowed me to bring the wine,"

she said before taking another sip.

"Why? Is this one not up to your standards? If not, I'll need to have a word with Betty, who recommended it for—and I quote—an evening in the bush." Sheryl plastered that crooked grin on her lips.

"It's perfect," Kristin said.

"Can I have a try?"

"Of course." Kristin offered Sheryl her glass.

Sheryl tipped the glass to her lips and took the tiniest of sips, after which she handed it back to Kristin immediately. "Well, if it's good enough for you." She blinked slowly, then leaned back in her chair, which creaked a little.

"My mother used to bring me here when I was a child," she said in a musing tone. "Used to say she would much prefer living here than in Campbelltown where I grew up."

"I guess I can see that." Kristin tried to look ahead as well, but she couldn't keep her gaze from shifting to Sheryl. She didn't want to interrupt Sheryl's impromptu moment of contemplation—seemingly brought about by that minute sip of wine—by reaching for a hunk of bread either, despite her stomach's insistent growl.

"For the longest time, that's what this cabin was to me. The place where I came with my mother. My father never joined. I don't know why. I never asked." A pause. "There are so many things I never got to ask."

"You, er, never see him?" Kristin couldn't imagine never seeing her parents. Despite their busy schedules, they were firmly rooted in her life.

"Not if I can help it." Sheryl righted her posture. "The man has been a very avid alcoholic for the past sixteen years, and he's not what I would call a sociable, agreeable drunk."

"Oh." Kristin tried to absorb that piece of information as quickly as she could in order to come up with a suitable reply. She wasn't fast enough.

"That's the reason I don't drink. I want to be nothing like him." Sheryl rubbed her palms on her jeans. "Anyway, enough gloomy talk. I didn't bring you here to tell you all about my dysfunctional family, I promise." The smile she shot Kristin was the least convincing one Kristin had seen on her.

"I'm very sorry to hear that." Kristin felt like she should say something, even though Sheryl suddenly seemed keen to end this particular conversation. "That you had to go through that." She put down her wineglass—she had to suppress the impulse to shove it all the way to the other end of the table—and brought her hand to Sheryl's knee.

"Just to be clear, I have absolutely no problem with you drinking, or being around people who drink. Being sober is my own, very personal choice and it should have no bearing on yours."

"Well, given the company I work for…" Kristin didn't know if the time was right for a half joke, but she tried anyway.

"I organize parties in my spare time. I was in charge of getting wine sponsorship. Really, it's a non-issue. It's not a hardship for me not to drink. I'm not a recovering addict. It's a choice, that's all." Sheryl shifted in her seat. "And, ironically, if it wasn't for wine, I wouldn't be sitting here with you." The palm she put on top of Kristin's hand was soft and tender.

Kristin had many more questions but didn't feel it was the right time to press for answers.

———

Sheryl hadn't meant to go all gloomy and nostalgic, though she should have anticipated it. Coming to the cabin always had the same effect on her. That was why she usually came here alone. Either way, she wouldn't be able to keep her family's dark secrets from Kristin forever, and a tiny glimpse now would, hopefully, inoculate Kristin against the real darkness that lurked in all the things still left unsaid.

"Let's eat," she said. But this meant letting go of Kristin's hand in hers, which she decidedly did not want to do. Though the sooner they ate, the sooner the time for other activities would roll around.

"Have you brought many women here?" Kristin inquired, after they filled their plates in silence.

"Only one." Sheryl heaped a piece of cheese onto a hunk of bread. "You." She hadn't meant it to sound so severe, but it was the truth. She'd certainly contemplated bringing girls here before, but something had always come up, either on her part or the other woman's. It was only now, with Kristin, that so easily, so suddenly, the stars had aligned and brought them here.

"I guess I'm flattered then."

"I'm flattered that you came."

"I didn't exactly know I was coming here, but for the record, I would have come anyway."

Sheryl couldn't stifle a laugh. "Touché. I lured you here."

"I wonder why." Kristin slid her plate away from her, indicating she was done eating.

"There's one thing in particular I wanted you to see. Give it another few hours, until darkness has totally fallen, and I'll take you to a small clearing over there." She pointed to the spot where her mother had first taken her years ago. "You don't see stars like that in the city."

Kristin quirked up her eyebrows and sucked her bottom lip between her teeth. "Whatever will we do to kill the time until the stars show up?"

"Wash some dishes perhaps." Sheryl didn't know why she suddenly got cold feet. Perhaps she'd shown a bit more of herself than she'd wanted already and it left her, for now, a little too insecure to play the part she liked to play. The forward one. The guiding force.

"How about we do those later?" Kristin pushed her chair back, rose, and took the few tiny steps needed to bridge the gap between them. "I can think of something so much better to do."

"I'm not objecting one bit."

"Good." Kristin bent down and kissed Sheryl fully on the lips. Her lips were so soft, so everything Sheryl had dreamed of as she sat on this very porch so often, looking out over the wonderful views, and feeling so alone—despite her many friends, acquaintances, and, even, lovers. A loneliness she never discussed, not even in her group of friends where no topic was off limits. In fact, the more taboo it was, the more you were encouraged to talk about it. Repression be damned—or in Aimee's words: "what you resist, persists." But for Sheryl, there was one thing she never mentioned. And it was the one thing that fed the deep, unshakable loneliness inside of her, in a way that, she sometimes believed, she had grown addicted to. The way her father had grown addicted to booze to alleviate the pain of losing her mother.

When they broke from the kiss, which was long and lingering, coming in waves, the intensity ratcheting up, then receding so they could suck some much-needed air into their lungs, Sheryl pushed herself out of her chair. She was of half a mind to curl an arm underneath Kristin's legs, swoop her up, and carry her to the bedroom. Even though they were the same height, Kristin seemed so much lighter than her, less bulky, easy to carry around like that.

"Let's go inside," she said, her voice breaking a little. Instead of picking Kristin up, she slung an arm around her waist and coaxed her to the bedroom.

The drive over here, the afternoon spent together, talking and wandering about the place, throwing rocks into the creek, followed by the dinner that Sheryl had kept intentionally light, had all led to this moment. The moment they both knew they were here for. They had been waiting for it all week, ever since Sheryl had asked if she could take Kristin somewhere. Though unspoken, they'd both known this was what it had been about. Of course, things could have turned out differently instead. In the clear light of day on Wednesday, when the afterglow of the party had truly settled, they could have looked at each other with doubt in their eyes. With too much trepidation for this burgeoning madness that was overtaking them. But perhaps Caitlin had been right. Perhaps this was a love-at-almost-first-sight whirlwind romance. The kind that, perhaps, only came along once in a lifetime, and they were both feeling the importance of it. Or, perhaps, Sheryl was in her head too much. Oh, she definitely was. Where was her gut instinct when she needed it most? And why did it seem to abandon her all over again?

"Everything okay?" Kristin whispered in her ear.

"Yes." Sheryl's voice sounded firm in a way that was hardly appropriate for the moment.

"You suddenly seem hesitant." Kristin came to stand in front of her.

"Trust me, I'm not." Sheryl became more infatuated with Kristin on the spot, just because she had asked. She gave her a wide smile, one that, she hoped, would take away all the hesitation she had displayed, and took a few more steps into the bedroom. It was just a bed, and a ramshackle one at that. Two nightstands on either side that Sheryl's grandfather had made himself. Two lamps that didn't resemble each other perched on top, of which Sheryl had no clue if they would still work. "I'm really, really not." She clasped her arms around Kristen's waist and found her neck with her lips.

––––––––

Kristin was already in seventh heaven. If Sheryl was having any doubts at all, she could easily guess the root of them. Kristin knew that any doubt in that bedroom wasn't born from unwillingness to do this but from the exact opposite. Too much will. Too much desire. She felt it beat under her skin, taking over her flesh. She felt like that bottle of wine Sheryl had brought for her. Kristin had opened it thirty minutes before she was going to drink it to let it breathe. Kristin had been breathing all day. She was ready to be consumed.

She felt Sheryl's lips on her neck, but also everywhere else. What was it about this woman that drove her so insane? She had a lot of confidence, sure, but, at times, it seemed brittle. Her blue eyes not only sparkled, but held a sadness as well. Maybe it wasn't only the effect Sheryl had on her because she was supposedly her type, but the combination of them being together. Maybe what Kristin was feeling at this very moment—extreme arousal shot through with hope —was only possible because she stood in this room, shaking on her legs, with Sheryl. Kristin was, in that moment, convinced that no one else could ever do that to her. Not so quickly, not leaving her so assured of everything that was to follow, not only in the next minutes but in the rest of their lives. And it was foolish and silly to think that way, but Kristin didn't give a damn. Pure lust rode up her spine, traveled through her flesh as Sheryl's lips kept connecting with her skin. It wasn't Kristin's first time as such, but it sure felt like it. Already, she was infinitely more aroused than all the times she'd been with Petra combined, and she and Sheryl were only kissing. No garments had come off. No intimate body parts had been bared.

"God, I want you," Sheryl murmured in her ear, and it set off another round of fireworks in Kristin's belly.

In response, Kristin started pulling her top over her head. She couldn't bear the feeling of being constrained by clothing any longer. She wanted to get naked, show herself, have Sheryl all over her, meet her anew as a lover, find out what made her tick. They had so much to learn about each other, not least of all what they liked in bed. Not that Kristin knew this about herself. She was easily pleased: she just wanted to be touched by another woman. Well, not just any woman—the way she had wrongly presumed before. She wanted to be touched by Sheryl. And she was. Sheryl's fingers drifted along her sides, up to her bra.

"Take it off," Kristin heard herself plead, unsure where

that sultry voice came from.

Sheryl unclasped the hooks and let Kristin's bra fall into her hands slowly, reverently, taking her time to reveal her breasts. Kristin didn't want her to take her time. She had a lifetime of missed sexual encounters to make up for. Thirty years was a long time to wait to be touched like this, by the right hands, by the right woman. At the same time, she wanted this to go slow, so she could luxuriate in every single second of it and never, ever forget about it.

Kristin started to unbutton Sheryl's shirt. When the top buttons were open, she was surprised to not find a bra underneath. She hadn't exactly been ogling Sheryl's chest all day, but she believed she would have noticed the woman she spent an entire day with being braless. She pushed her lack of observational skills to the back of her mind and focused on what she saw. Sheryl's breasts slowly being revealed. Kristin quickly understood the appeal of a slow revelation. Between her legs, where something had been steadily pulsing with anticipation, the rhythm had just picked up speed again.

Then there they stood. Naked from the waist up. Face-to-face. Two women who had only spoken on the telephone a short week ago. How quickly things could change. How the course of her life could be altered so drastically by one moment of bravery. Kristin reached for the button of Sheryl's jeans, then let Sheryl slide them off her legs herself. Apparently, she hadn't gone commando entirely throughout the day, because a pair of red panties were revealed. Kristin hadn't expected the brazen color and the seductive cut, but what did she know?

She pushed her own pants down. The linen slid off her legs easily and crumpled into a heap on the floor.

"Come on." Sheryl took her hand and together they walked the one step that removed them from the bed. They sat, awkwardly for a split second, until passion overrode all other emotions again, and they pressed their lips together as they tumbled down, their limbs all tangled up, onto the bed.

Kristin felt every kiss in every cell of her body—and she hoped to soak up some of Sheryl's experience by kissing osmosis.

When they broke apart, Sheryl, lying half on top of her, said, "I'm so glad you came to that party."

"I'm so glad you were in charge of booze."

The skin around Sheryl's eyes crinkled as she smiled down at her. The air grew silent around them. Serious. Sheryl leaned in and kissed her again, and this time, because of their state of undress and their position on the bed, it ignited a much fiercer round of fireworks in Kristin's belly. She was ready to lose herself to this woman. To give herself up the way she'd never done before. It was time. And there was no doubt in her mind that she would, despite this being their first time.

As Sheryl's lips kept landing on hers, and her tongue slipped into her mouth, soft and sweet, Kristin was certain of so many things she had no right to be. She was a girl overflowing with common sense, with a clear head set upon her shoulders, who didn't believe in things like this, until she lay kissing, half-naked, with Sheryl on the bed in a cabin in the mountains.

Sheryl's lips shifted to her cheek, then trailed a moist path down her neck, to finally stop at her breasts. Before taking one of Kristin's peaked nipples in her mouth, she looked at it as though she had just unwrapped the greatest gift she'd ever received. When her lips did finally close around it, Kristin felt the their soft touch spread through her entire body, as though her blood had been set alight, and the touch of Sheryl's tongue against her nipple was the match that had lit it.

Sheryl divided her attention between both nipples and with one hand, kneaded Kristin's small breasts, lifting them higher to her lips, drinking her in.

She then lowered her attention, tracing her tongue to Kristin's belly button, which she circled and flew right past, on her way down.

Kristin's clit pulsed hard against the fabric of her panties. How could she be so aroused so quickly already? Petra had never been able to do that to her. Then she stopped wondering about the how, and surrendered to the now, because Sheryl's lips kissed a path along the waistband of her panties. Then her tongue followed the same line, moistening Kristin's skin as she felt her pussy grow wetter and wetter.

Kristin felt a finger flit along the panel of her panties, light and enticing. A split second later, her swollen lips were exposed to the air as Sheryl's finger drew her panties down, pulling them off her in a swift movement.

Kristin's muscles tensed for a beat, then relaxed. What if this was the first time with the woman she would spend the rest of her life with? How significant did that make this moment of baring it all?

Kristin lost her train of thought again when she felt Sheryl's finger, for the very first time, run along the length of her nether lips.

Kristin delved her fingers in Sheryl's hair while she let her legs fall farther apart. For Sheryl, she wanted to spread herself as wide as possible, make her feel as welcome as she could.

Sheryl's finger flitted lightly over her lips, circled her clit, which was ready to explode with anticipation. They hadn't talked much about Sheryl's former lovers, but everything about her exuded a sort of confidence that Kristin believed could only come with vast experience. Sheryl knew how to touch a woman, that much was certain, and Kristin was a woman who had waited a very long time to be touched. In that respect, they were already perfect for each other.

It wasn't just Sheryl's exploring finger causing Kristin's heartbeat to skyrocket. It was, perhaps even more so, the position of her head and where it indicated her gaze was fixed.

For a split second, Kristin wondered whether Sheryl was part of a group at university that huddled together in a circle and got their hand mirrors out to look at their nether regions, as an act of self-love or whatever they called it. Sheryl kind of struck her as the type. It came with the assuredness she displayed, and the light but deft touch with which her finger moved all over her, now applying some more pressure, its tip slipping slowly inside of her.

Kristin bucked up her hips in anticipation. Somehow feeling Sheryl's finger slide inside of her represented the pinnacle of this lovely day they had spent together. Perhaps Kristin would come, perhaps she wouldn't—she didn't have enough experience to predict the outcome—but it didn't matter, because this moment, the one in which Sheryl, with a brand-new sense of determination about her, slid high inside of her, was already everything.

Sheryl's lips touched down on her skin again. Her tongue shot down. Another finger was added. Kristin had been so wrong. All her senses were flooded with exquisite sensation. The smell of the trees outside mixed with the scent of her urgent arousal. Sheryl's one hand on her belly, the fingers of the other inside of her. The sight of Sheryl's head moving gently up and down. And then, the best of everything, Sheryl's tongue on her clit.

"Oh Jesus Christ," Kristin moaned. Sheryl's fingers kept delving, causing a delicious tingle to run through her with every thrust, but what was really doing her in was Sheryl's tongue flicking over her clit like that. She'd gone from gentle to frantic in a matter of seconds and Kristin felt it everywhere.

Something inside of her belly started contracting, then spread to her sex, and though fully expected, the intensity of it surprised Kristin. She got a sense she was howling profanities but was deaf to the sound of her own voice as the climax tore through her. The very first orgasm delivered by Sheryl's hands. God, those hands. The thought of them caused another ripple of pleasure to wash all over her. The ripples kept on coming, zapping all the energy from her, leaving her limbs loose and muscles drained.

Sheryl crawled up to her, peppering her cheek and neck with the lightest of kisses, then gazing down at her again, the way she had done before her excursion south. There was a different kind of sparkle in the blue of her eyes. Perhaps caused by the shifting light outside, or perhaps by something else. Either way, Kristin interpreted it as the two of them being on the exact same page: the first one of their long history together.

CHAPTER SEVEN

"Hey." No matter how many times she'd woken up in this very bed, Sheryl always seemed to forget the racket the birds made at first light—which came at an ungodly hour at this time of the year. When she'd opened her eyes a beat earlier, she'd found Kristin awake and looking at her already. "Sorry about nature's alarm clock."

"Don't be. It's magnificent," Kristin said. "It reminds me I should get out of the city more."

"It would be even more magnificent if they kept it down until at least after six o'clock." Sheryl theatrically flopped her pillow from under her head and pressed it to her ears.

"Don't be such a drama queen." Kristin shuffled closer to her, her warm body pressing against Sheryl's underneath the sheets.

"No one has ever accused me of being that before." Sheryl looked at Kristin from underneath the pillow. At her sleep-crusted eyes, and the way the skin around her temples wrinkled ever so lightly. Crows' feet so light, they were probably only visible in this light. Perhaps only at this particular time of the day, when the birds were chirping, and Sheryl's eyesight might have gotten a boost from the massive orgasm she'd had only a few hours earlier.

"There's a first time for everything then." Kristin pried the pillow from between Sheryl's fingers.

"Oh yes," Sheryl said, "there most certainly is."

"Anyway, it serves you right. You shouldn't have kept us up half the night with your... shenanigans." Sheryl could feel Kristin's breath on her cheek.

"Is that what you call it? Shenanigans?" In one fluid motion, Sheryl pushed herself off her side and on to Kristin, her knee pressing between her legs.

"How do you call it in the Gender Studies department? Making sweet, sweet love?"

You would never know by looking at her, but Kristin had a sharp sense of humor hidden underneath that proper exterior of hers. And all the things she had shown Sheryl last night. If anything, it was Sheryl who felt she'd been left behind by Kristin's abandon. Sheryl with her years of experience, who was out and proud, and who had at least one discussion about the female orgasm every week.

Perhaps Sheryl had been too ambitious in wanting to add the gravitas this cabin gave to her actions. The memories she had here, though certainly not all good, were of such nostalgic force that they couldn't be ignored. She'd been a fool to have tried. She also knew that there was only one way to dispel the power the cabin still held over her. She had to tell Kristin. She kissed her on both cheeks, then slid off Kristin's body, keeping an arm slung around her waist.

"We mostly just call it fucking," Sheryl said, knowing how blunt that sounded.

"How lovely." Kristin was still smiling.

"We can hardly call it intercourse when that doesn't apply to a big percentage of people."

"So *fucking* is the politically correct way of calling it?"

"It sure is." How was Sheryl even going to broach the subject? She couldn't say something like that while they were lounging in bed—and, quite possibly, about to fuck again.

"I would never have guessed. Good thing I have you now to school me in all things PC." Kristin ran her nails over Sheryl's arm. "Good thing indeed."

"How about some breakfast?" Sheryl asked.

Kristin shrugged. "Depends. Do I need to go outside and pick my own berries?" She clasped her fingers around

Sheryl's forearm. A sign Sheryl couldn't—and didn't want to —misinterpret.

"You are a princess here. You don't have to do a thing."

"I do hope that's a declaration of intent for the rest of our affair."

Sheryl chuckled while being very aware of the warmth spreading through her flesh at the mention of the *rest of their affair*. "I mean *here*, in this cabin only, of course."

"I guess we'll have to move here then once we— inevitably—move in together next month."

Sheryl laughed out loud. There was a lightness to Kristin, not only to her physical body, but to her spirit, that drew her in. Perhaps it was the sort of lightness that came with living a charmed life, which for Sheryl, was a life with two parents who loved you and were there for you.

"I guess I'm more than you bargained for when you told me I was on the guest list for the LAUS party." Kristin rolled on her side, facing Sheryl.

"So much more." Sheryl kissed her on the tip of the nose. "You're a true delight, the likes of which I haven't encountered in a long while, maybe forever."

"And you're such a natural charmer."

They kissed and Sheryl forgot about what she wanted to tell Kristin, though, of course, it was a thing she could never truly forget about, no matter how many delightful women she kissed.

———

Sheryl brewed coffee in the ancient coffeemaker. Surely it couldn't be the same one that her mother had used when they came here together, but somehow her memories had blended together so that Sheryl believed it was. Her mother had pressed that button and the cabin had filled with the smell of coffee long before Sheryl had tasted it.

She watched the water drip slowly into the filter. Kristin was in the shower, giving Sheryl time to lay out breakfast and contemplate *why* she wanted to tell Kristin. Why it felt like a hurdle she needed to jump over in order for the relationship she wanted to have with Kristin to be true. Perhaps being surrounded by self-proclaimed truth speakers for most waking hours of her life hadn't missed its effect.

"I like the smell of that." Kristin walked out of the bathroom, a towel wrapped around her.

"And I like the sight of that." Sheryl felt a tenderness wash over her. An inclination to move forward, not only physically—as in take a few steps into Kristin's direction—but forward with everything. She made a pact with herself that, before she allowed herself to touch Kristin, whose freshly-showered body held so much appeal, again, she'd have to tell her. She'd have to give up this crucial part of her. She'd have to share her burden. She squared her shoulders, as though the mere act of doing so could chase away the breaking waves of lust in her blood. But they were forging a connection, a bond not easily broken.

"Come sit outside with me?" Sheryl asked. "The berries are picked and breakfast is ready."

When they sat, side by side, overlooking the vista in the golden morning light, Sheryl was struck by the beauty of everything, as if the same view she'd seen a hundred times had suddenly amplified its attractiveness. She could also hear Caitlin's voice in her head: *Oh, what pheromones can do to you.*

"When I came here with my mother, she always sat right here, in this very chair," Sheryl started. "When I was a child, I didn't care much for the view. I was just running around between the trees, trying to get my mom to play with me, but she wasn't really the playing type. She'd just sit here, smoking, watching over me."

"How old were you when she died?"

"Twelve." Sheryl tried to keep her voice free of tremors. She stared straight ahead. At the same tree her mother used to stare at endlessly. "She killed herself. It ruined my dad. Me as well a little, I guess."

"Oh no." Kristin turned toward her. "I'm so sorry."

Sheryl kept looking ahead, but she felt Kristin's gaze on her. "It was a long time ago. They didn't tell me it was suicide at first. I only found out when my father blurted it out in a drunken fit a day before the funeral."

"Jesus." Kristin shuffled in her seat.

Sheryl felt the lightest touch of a hand on her knee. "I didn't believe him at first. I didn't believe my mother would leave me like that. I couldn't understand why she would do that." Sheryl believed she wasn't doing such a bad job of recounting the facts. Her hands remained steady, her voice calm. "Officially, I lived with my father, but my Aunt Rita stepped in a lot. She came round all the time, often took me home with her, fed me, bought me a new school uniform once in a while." She shrugged. "All things considered, I turned out all right."

"My goodness, Sheryl. No child should go through something like that."

"Yet children go through so many things." Sheryl finally turned to face Kristin. "Many through much worse than I did."

Kristin shook her head. "It's good that you told me." She reached for Sheryl's hand and held it firmly between hers.

"It's not something I go around shouting off rooftops, as you can imagine. Not many people know this about me, but ever since we arrived here yesterday, I've felt compelled to tell you. To explain myself to you better. Not to gain your sympathy. But I needed you to know this about me."

Kristin nodded. "This place must be full of memories."

"It was an impulsive decision to bring you here, but it felt right." Sheryl squeezed Kristin's hand. "So many things about you feel right."

"I know that feeling." Kristin brought their hands to her mouth and planted a soft peck on one of Sheryl's knuckles. "I feel like I should tell you something dreadful that happened to me in my childhood, but I was a pampered only child of Korean immigrants. My parents' only fault is that they can't really fathom the fact that their daughter might be a lesbian. It seems so foolish now. I feel foolish for not telling them."

"We all have our own cross to bear."

"Perhaps, but some are heavier than others."

"You don't have to tell me anything. This isn't a quid pro quo. I just didn't want this to be something I would tell you in a few weeks' time. Didn't want it to be something I had kept from you. But that's all it is. As I said, I think I turned out rather well."

"You turned out one fine woman." If Kristin scooted any closer, she'd be sitting on Sheryl's lap. "Can I ask a follow-up question?"

"Sure."

"You never see your father?"

Sheryl felt her muscles deflate. "I haven't seen him in years. I had to let him go, for my own sanity. I tried taking care of him for a long time, but nothing I ever did helped. When Mom died, he disappeared as well. He checked out." Sheryl decided to keep that particular, equally painful conversation for another time. Out of sight was definitely not out of mind. She thought of her father often, of that shell of a man, drinking the rest of his life away. "I think I'm ready to change the subject now." She tried a smile but didn't manage to pull her lips all the way into one convincingly. "Let's talk about you now."

CHAPTER EIGHT

Kristin didn't know how to keep a straight face, how to not communicate all these things she felt blazing inside of her to her parents, who were still the people who knew her best. Not in all ways, of course, but surely, in more ways than Kristin felt comfortable contemplating.

There she sat, opposite them, in the apartment where she had grown up. If she went down the hall and opened the door to her room, she would find it intact, nothing altered, as though her mother felt the need to keep it as a shrine to the dream of the daughter she knew she would never have.

One weekend and everything seemed to have changed, even the way she carried herself around her parents. How was this *Don't Ask, Don't Tell* policy going to work now? So far, it had been easy. Kristin had, literally, had nothing to tell them. As if being a lesbian was only true if she were having sex, which was a ridiculous notion. But it was also a very comfortable safety blanket to hide beneath all these years she had known, but never said.

In their family dynamic, it was more important to be kind than to be completely truthful, and in this particular instance, kindness translated into omitting some crucial facts about herself, despite them being inherently understood. Kristin's parents were no fools, but tradition still weighed heavy on them, even though they had left Korea a very long time ago—or perhaps that was why they attached more importance to it, because of the connection to their motherland it still offered.

Either way, it was only tradition in spirit. They were

always enlightened enough to not make any futile demands of Kristin, didn't think their own wish to see their daughter marry a decent Korean man more important than their daughter's happiness. So, in that, Kristin considered herself lucky also.

They had the obligatory miyeok guk and made polite conversation the way they always did. Kristin inquired about her parents' jobs and they about hers. They feasted on half a bottle of Korean plum wine, even though Kristin had brought a bottle of Sauvignon Blanc, if only for herself. But she always drank the beverage her mother served. She didn't know why exactly, though she was sure that, subconsciously, it had something to do with the wish to comply, to obey. Which, come to think of it, sounded like something Sheryl would say. Kristin would never be able to keep Sheryl a secret if it felt as though she was going everywhere with her.

"I'll get the birthday cake," her father offered and disappeared into the kitchen. Kristin hadn't received a gift-wrapped present. Instead, she knew that when she checked her savings account tomorrow, the same amount as every year would have been deposited into it. Her parents were practical people and had, long ago, forsaken the habit of finding a suitable gift for their daughter's birthday. Kristin knew that, despite always making the effort of buying each one of them something small and inexpensive enough not to seem wasteful of money, she couldn't give her parents a better gift than showing them a bank statement of the growing amount in her savings account.

To Kristin's surprise, the cake was not the same old pavlova her mother made from scratch every year. This year, because it was a special birthday, she'd bought a chocolate mirror cake with an outside layer so shiny, Kristin could make out her own reflection in it. What would she see if she looked into an actual mirror right now, as she celebrated her thirtieth birthday with her parents? Would she see a happy woman? Yes, she would, Kristin concluded. So why could that happiness not be shared with the people who, she presumed, wanted to see her happy most in the world? Or was the happiness they wanted for her so tangled up with their own expectations and hopes and dreams that Kristin was not allowed her own individual style of happiness? Her own desires? And wasn't that the most ludicrous notion of all?

Keeping up appearances was not on Kristin's to-do list for her birthday party. It simply couldn't be. It was a milestone birthday. Thirty years ago, her mother, who had come to this country as a mere adolescent on a student visa, had given birth to her, had made Kristin's life possible. So didn't she owe it to the labor her mother had gone through, not just on that day but all the ones coming before and after, to share this new happiness she had found? One more profound than she had ever encountered before in her adult life, where birthdays had become a reminder of all the things she hadn't yet done?

Kristin's mother cut the cake. She offered a big portion to Kristin, while only cutting a thin slice for herself and Kristin's father. This was usually the time when Kristin's father would say a few words expressing his pride in her. Kristin remembered the elaborate speeches he used to deliver when she was in her early teens, and how she'd sat beaming in the gloriousness of his words, still too young to be aware of the many expectations it heaped on her.

Instead of speaking, her father fixed his eyes on her and gazed at her intently—the way he would look at one of his patients, Kristin knew, because her father was still her GP when it came to trivial matters like a cold. For more intimate medical matters, she'd found someone outside the family a long time ago.

"There's something different about you," Kristin's father said.

"She looks like she spent too much time in the sun without applying sunscreen," her mother, the dermatologist, said.

Kristin hated it when they spoke about her in the third person, as though she wasn't even there. But old habits were hard to break. Her parents had done this for as long as she could remember. As though their daughter was an asset to be discussed—to be valued.

"I went to the Blue Mountains last weekend," she said. She almost added "with a friend", but Sheryl was already so much more than a friend. Calling her that would diminish what they had, and that was the opposite of what Kristin wanted to do. She wanted to honor their connection, their *coup de foudre,* that special something they shared.

"With whom?" her mother was quick to ask.

"Her name is Sheryl and…" Kristin knew that any hesitation at this crucial moment would allow either one of them to make a dismissive remark that would make her veer off course, but it was so hard to say it. What would she even call Sheryl? Her girlfriend? They had met barely ten days ago.

"I'll get some more tea." Her mother was in the process of rising from the table already.

"Mom, no, please sit." She couldn't let her flee. It didn't matter that Kristin didn't have a label to stick on Sheryl yet. It did matter that Kristin was head-over-heels in love, of course it did, but it didn't change anything about who, at her very core, she was and had always been.

"Her name is Sheryl and she's not just a friend." There. She'd said it. Damn it. A blush heated up her cheeks, despite this being one of the proudest moments of her life.

"I think I will get that tea now." Her mother rose again.

"Get us something stronger while you're at it," her father said.

Kristin didn't know what to say while her mother hurried into the kitchen and clattered dishes about. She and her father sat in silence, waiting for her mother to return, as though only then another word might be spoken.

Kristin's pulse thudded beneath her skin. It was a relief

to have said what she'd just said out loud, but it also changed the careful balancing act she and her parents had been performing ever since Kristin had told them to no longer push her to date the sons of their friends. In a way, this was her second coming out. She wondered how many more she would need to do until it truly sunk in.

The first one hadn't been as intentional as this one. It had just been a request uttered in an uncharacteristically impolite fashion, which always made Kristin's parents sit up and take note. And it had worked. They had ceased their endless nudges toward her dating this or that boy, reciting the boy in question's many accomplishments, which, more often than not, included him being about to graduate from law school or med school. Once they had tried pushing a mere accountant on her, though pushing wasn't the correct word for it either—it was just how Kristin perceived it. It was more subtle than that, and it had taken Kristin a couple of years to realize that when they spoke of Mrs Kim's son in encouraging ways, it wasn't just because they liked him as a person and admired his accomplishments.

Kristin knew that for this coming out to be effective, she might have to be clearer, might actually have to spell it out to them, to these two highly intelligent people.

"In fact," she said, as her mother returned with a bottle of soju, "I would like you to meet her."

Her mother banged the bottle onto the table, shocking herself, apparently. She brought a hand to her mouth.

"If that's what you want, then we will," her father said. He looked at her mother, trying to find her gaze, but her mother had her eyes cast down, inspecting her hands in her lap.

"What does she do?" her father asked.

Kristin knew she shouldn't think like that, but she was so glad that Sheryl had gainful employment of a certain stature. "She's a post-grad student getting her PhD in Gender Studies," she said.

"Gender studies?" her mother asked. "You mean sociology?"

"Here's an idea," Kristin said, "why don't you invite her over and she can explain it all herself."

"Hm," her mother grunted.

Her father poured a tiny amount of liquor into three glasses and distributed them around the table. He held his up, looked Kristin straight in the eye, and said, "I look forward to meeting Sheryl."

———

"They want to meet me?" Sheryl asked. "The people who held you hostage all evening long on your thirtieth birthday, preventing me from celebrating with you."

"I'm here now." It was barely nine o'clock. Kristin had rushed over to Sheryl's apartment after the dinner at her parents. "We have all night."

"All night would have been me taking you to a fancy restaurant, ordering a bottle of champagne, and hand-feeding you spoonfuls of caviar."

"Don't be ridiculous. You're hardly the type to do any of these things."

"You don't know that." Sheryl smiled warmly.

"Either way, it's a pity you don't have any champagne in the house, because not only is today my birthday, but I also came out to my parents *and* I haven't been disowned."

"This goes to show just how little you know me." Sheryl walked to the fridge and produced a half bottle of champagne. "All the way from France, for my lady."

Kristin walked over to her and threw her arms around Sheryl's neck. "Do you have caviar in there as well?"

Sheryl shook her head. "I have to draw the line somewhere." She pulled Kristin into a closer embrace. "Congratulations on a successful coming out. I'll be on my best behavior when we meet."

"It would have been better if you were a doctor or a lawyer."

"Once I finish my PhD I will be a doctor."

"I'm not sure they fully understand what it is you're getting your PhD in."

"That's something we can sympathize over then. I'm not always sure myself," Sheryl joked.

Kristin laughed. The sound of happiness reverberated through Sheryl's tiny apartment.

"Are you, er, okay with meeting them? It's not too soon and…" A pause.

"And what?" Sheryl handed her a glass of champagne. She'd poured a tiny amount into a glass for herself.

"I'll tell them in advance not to ask about your parents."

Sheryl held up her glass. "I can handle any questions that come my way."

"I'm sure you can, but what I'm trying to say is that if you want to talk about it, I'm here. Perhaps meeting my parents will stir up some unwanted memories for you."

"First, certain issues should not be discussed on your birthday." There was a sharpness to Sheryl's tone that Kristin hadn't heard before. "I told you about my mother and father because I wanted you to have that information, not because I want to discuss it. I've had the required therapy. I've done all the talking I want to do about it." The hint of hardness disappeared from her face. "I appreciate your concern, I really do. But it's unnecessary. I'm a big girl, one who doesn't dwell in the past. And I don't mean to brag, but parents usually love me."

Kristin swallowed all the questions that burned in her mind. She had many, and they'd only grown since they'd returned from the cabin, but if Sheryl didn't want to talk about it, then she wasn't going to push her. If anything, Kristin felt honored that Sheryl had confided in her, had shown her vulnerability so quickly and so openly. She clinked the rim of her champagne glass against Sheryl's.

"I'm sure you'll charm the pants off them." She took a

sip. "Exactly how many girlfriends have taken you to meet their parents?"

Sheryl smirked. "Only one. And they were completely besotted with me."

Kristin wasn't keen on interrogating Sheryl on her past girlfriends on her birthday. She'd keep that conversation for another time.

"This stuff isn't half bad," Sheryl said, and swallowed the liquid in her glass in one go. "And no, I don't think it's too soon for me to meet your parents. I think it will be good for them to meet me, if only to put their mind at ease that I'm not some vixen from hell who has seduced their daughter to cross over to the dyke side."

Kristin chuckled.

"Happy birthday," Sheryl said, put their glasses to the side, and pulled Kristin close.

CHAPTER NINE

"Monogamy all the way for you?" Caitlin asked Sheryl.

Sheryl shook her head in despair. She should have known. "I don't want to be with anyone else."

"I don't know, Sher." Caitlin leaned back in her seat, tipping a glass of wine to her lips, not a hint of hesitation about what she was about to say on her face. "You seem kind of pussy-whipped to me."

"What are you talking about?"

"You're meeting her parents. You told her about your family. What's next? Shall I call the moving company, or do you want to do that yourself?"

"We're in love. What's so bad about that?"

"Oh, nothing at all, but, hm, don't you think everything is moving a tad too fast?"

Sometimes, Sheryl wished she had the sort of friends who didn't feel the need to analyze everything and could just be happy for her. "What is too fast, really? Maybe what is fast for you is slow for me. Everyone is different. Besides, I clearly remember someone telling me not long ago that this might be the one, that you just never know."

"Guilty as charged, but I just don't want you to rush into something and end up hurt. That's all."

"You don't get it, Caitlin—"

Caitlin held up a hand. "Please don't say what I think you're about to say, being that I don't get it because I've never felt this way."

"Would I ever say something like that?" Sheryl shot her friend a big smile. "What I was trying to say before being rudely interrupted, is that *I know*. And which one of my dear friends was it again who coined that phrase? I do wonder. It must have been a wise woman, that's for sure."

"Well if *you're* meeting her parents, I demand to meet *her*."

"You will. Soon enough." It wasn't as if Sheryl hadn't considered the swiftness with which she was falling for Kristin. She was all in already, which wasn't her usual M.O.— and which was probably the reason why Caitlin was calling her out on it. Sheryl wasn't the head-over-heels type. At least, she thought she wasn't. Perhaps, if the right woman came along, she was. She wondered if she would have noticed Kristin at the party if someone else had been in charge of wine sponsorship—if she had allowed her past to keep her from taking on that particular task. Perhaps she would have been too busy to notice Kristin. Or her heart would have started beating faster as she applied the stamp after letting her in. Or, and this was perhaps most probable of all the things that didn't happen, Kristin might not have come to the party at all. The sponsorship procurer might not have flirted with Kristin the way Sheryl had, and nothing would have happened. Kristin would still be in the closet. And Sheryl's heart wouldn't be all the way in her throat as it was now, even when she was just talking about Kristin.

"I'm nervous," Kristin admitted.

"I really couldn't tell. You keep fiddling with that bracelet and your knees must be having a ball hopping up and down like that," Sheryl said.

"That's not helping."

"I know, but you have nothing to be nervous about."

"What if I'm not feminist enough for them?"

"What if I'm *too* feminist for Cassie?"

"Don't worry about Cassie. You'll blow her away."

"Why would the same not be true in your case? Besides, Caitlin and Betty might not have officially met you yet, but they clocked you at the LAUS party. Trust me, your presence there did not go unnoticed."

"Why? Because uptight Koreans stick out like sore thumbs at lesbian parties?"

Sheryl laughed and shook her head. "Trust me when I tell you that you are far from uptight."

"But I'm not like you and, presumably, not like your friends."

"Caitlin might give a speech on how monogamy is not built into our DNA and how it's against evolution and all that, but that doesn't mean she won't like you. Though it might mean that you won't like her." Sheryl looked up. "Speak of the devil." She bent over the table and whispered to Kristin. "And sometimes that can be taken quite literally." She plastered a big smile on her face, rose, and hugged Caitlin as she kissed her on each cheek.

What a greeting, Kristin thought. She and Cassie just nodded at each other when they met up. Christ, she needed another glass of Merlot. Kristin didn't know how Sheryl got through situations like these without the lubricating effects of alcohol. She herself was living proof that drinking alcohol didn't have to lead to abuse.

By the time she was introduced to Caitlin, Betty and her girlfriend had arrived as had Cassie. Kristin couldn't help but wonder how it made Cassie feel to have drinks with a bunch of lesbians. It wasn't that long ago that they both had been, to Cassie's knowledge, two straight best friends. That was the thing about coming out. It changed the lives of those around you as well.

Wine was poured generously, pleasantries exchanged, and Kristin soon learned she truly shouldn't have been nervous. Sheryl had a way of putting not only her but the people around them at ease. Soon Betty's girlfriend was talking to Cassie, Betty and Sheryl engaged in a back-and-forth about the meaning of something their mutual boss Aimee had said, which left Kristin to engage Caitlin in conversation. She knew Caitlin and Sheryl had dated briefly once, which intimidated her further, but as it turned out, Caitlin was much like Sheryl and had refined the art of skipping awkward small talk and launching into a big topic headfirst.

"I see you shave your legs," she said, leaning back and examining Kristin's body below her skirt.

"Er, yes," Kristin said.

"What's your motivation?"

Kristin quirked up her eyebrows. "What do you mean?"

"Do you shave them to conform to what society—and by society I mainly mean the male gaze—expects of you or just simply for your own esthetic reasons?"

"I have quite honestly never thought about that." Kristin vaguely remembered her mother putting a razor in the palm of her hand and showing her how to rid her legs of hair. She'd seen her mother do it, then she was doing it herself. She had never questioned why her father didn't go through the ordeal—because it could surely feel like that from time to time.

"If you do think about it, you will find that there are many things women do, just out of habit, or because we've been doing it for such a long time, that men don't."

"I just like the feel of smooth skin." Kristin didn't quite know what to say.

"That might be so, but if you hadn't started shaving in the first place, your skin would still be smooth regardless."

Sheryl turned her head toward them, one eyebrow cocked up.

"Your speech has come fifteen years too late, Caitlin," she said, slapping her friend on the shoulder. "She gave me the same one when we first met. I've since told her many times to work on her opening lines."

Caitlin waved her off. "The little things are important. It's only by changing small things that bigger things will shift."

"I agree with you wholeheartedly," Sheryl said. "But this is not a LAUS gathering, nor a department meeting."

"I'm just getting to know Kristin better," Caitlin said. "This is my way."

"You could try letting her get a word in edgewise," Sheryl teased. "I hear it's really helpful to let people speak when you want to get to know them."

Kristin enjoyed the banter. The ease between them. How Caitlin rolled her eyes and said, "Next you're going to tell me this is why I'm single while you know very well I'm not looking for a relationship. In fact—" She turned her attention back to Kristin. "Did you know that monogamy —"

"Stop!" Sheryl shouted. "You said the M-word. How long have we been sitting here?" She looked at her watch ostentatiously. "Not even half an hour."

Caitlin bent over the table and whispered to Kristin. "I only said it to wind her up. She's so easy." She threw in a wink, and just like that, a deeper rapport was forged between Kristin and Sheryl's best friend.

"I hear you're taking Sheryl to meet your parents," Caitlin said, after Sheryl had picked up her conversation with Betty again.

Kristin watched Sheryl from the corner of her eye, took in the way she gestured her hands as she spoke, eager to make a point. Warmth spread through her body as she watched Sheryl speak. There was so much to learn about another person just by hearing them talk to a friend. All Kristin saw in that moment was Sheryl's kindness, her willingness to listen, her eagerness to joke, her way of explaining. There was no sign of the other Sheryl that must be hiding somewhere deep inside. The abandoned twelve-year-old. The hurt teenager who had to make sense of a world without her mother.

"Earth to Kristin," Caitlin said, waving a hand in front of Kristin's face. "Good grief, I get you're in love, but must you really be staring at her like that?" She chuckled and leaned over the table again. "But, yeah, I get it. She's a real stunner, isn't she?"

A blush crept up Kristin's cheeks, heated up her neck. "She swept me off my feet."

"You did the same to her," Caitlin said.

Kristin's blush intensified.

———

"They loved you," Sheryl said. "Which is completely understandable."

They were walking home from the bar to Sheryl's flat, where they always ended up staying. Sheryl had only been to Kristin's place once, after she'd dropped her off on their way back from the cabin. Sheryl had declared Kristin's apartment looked ready to be photographed for the new Ikea catalog.

"I'll get the down-low on what Cassie thought of you soon enough. It must be weird for her because she's never actually seen me with another woman."

"I hope my crowd was not too rowdy for her."

"Rowdiness is not much of an issue for Cassie." Kristin stopped, tugged at Sheryl's sleeve. "I'm not very experienced, which is why I'm wondering. Is this how it's supposed to go? Is this what really falling in love feels like?"

"What *do* you feel?" Sheryl came to stand in front of her, head slanted, something sparkling in her eyes. "Just so that I can confirm."

Kristin chuckled. She took a moment to gather her thoughts and translate them into words that could actually be said. "Like, for the first time ever, everything is falling into place. Everything is right. Meeting your friends tonight was right. You being about to meet my parents is right. Like it should be. Us walking along the street on the way to your apartment is right."

Sheryl stepped a little closer. "Just right?" Kristin could feel her breath on her skin. "Not spectacular? Or so right you feel your heart could burst out of your chest any moment, just because it's beating for all the right reasons?"

"You have a fondness for hyperbole." Kristin kissed Sheryl on the cheek.

"Or maybe just a more expressive way of explaining my feelings."

"As well as a desire to always have the last word." Kristin gazed into Sheryl's eyes.

Sheryl quirked up her eyebrows but didn't say anything.

"What?" Kristin asked.

"Nothing, just proving a point," Sheryl said before kissing Kristin fully on the mouth, in the middle of the sidewalk.

CHAPTER TEN

"She doesn't drink?" Kristin's mother repeated.

"No."

"Oh." She twirled the bottle of red wine around in her hands. "So I should put this away?"

"No, it's fine. We can drink. Sheryl just isn't much of a drinker." It suddenly struck Kristin that Sheryl was about to see her very origin. That she would look at her mother and father and could try to piece the puzzle of Kristin together. Kristin would never be able to do that with Sheryl. She would never actually see where she came from.

"Of course we can't. We can't have a guest in our house and sit around drinking alcohol while she doesn't drink." It also struck Kristin that her mother might be very nervous about this. She hadn't asked much about Sheryl. She had just inquired about her dietary habits and was only then, fifteen minutes before Sheryl was about to arrive—and Kristin hoped feverishly that she would be on time, which, she had already learned, wasn't always the case with Sheryl—asking about which wine to serve, Shiraz or Merlot?

"Mom, I'm telling you it's fine. If anything, *you* look like you could do with a drink."

"Is she a recovering alcoholic? Because then it would truly be insensitive."

"No, she's not. You should be happy. In his practice, Dad is always advising people to drink less. Sheryl will drink a small glass to be polite, if she feels like it, but that's it. She just doesn't like alcohol." Kristin sympathized with Sheryl more. So many social situations, out of sheer habit, revolved around drinking. The flack she must get for refusing. And how strange that it was so uncommon for people to do so.

"Okay, if you say so. And yes, I think I might have a glass. Would you like one?"

"Sure."

Kristin waited by her mother's side while she poured the wine. Her father was out on the deck, lighting the barbecue. For some reason, they believed they had to serve Sheryl Australia's national dish, despite nearly always having Korean food when they ate alone.

"Cheers." Kristin sought her mother's gaze when she clinked the belly of her wineglass against hers, but it was kept from her. Which made her realize that it was a good thing this was happening so fast, lest her parents intentionally forgot their daughter was a lesbian again. They had to see it with their own eyes to actually believe it was true. If not, a residue of hope would always remain. Hope for a big Korean wedding. For grandchildren. For their child not to be discriminated against, Kristin guessed. At least, that's what Sheryl had told her. "Nine times out of ten, it's not disapproval but fear that keeps parents from freely accepting their children's sexual preference."

They drank in silence, her mother nervously clattering about, adjusting the position of the cutlery on the dining table. It was a beautiful summer night and they could have easily eaten outside, but for some unvoiced reason, her mother had deemed that inappropriate and set the table in the dining room.

Kristin knocked her glass of wine back more eagerly than she was used to. She had confidence in Sheryl being gracious and charming, but not so much in her parents, to whom this was all new. It was new to her as well.

———

To Sheryl's surprise, it was Kristin's father who was the real stunner. Dr. Park was a tall man with impossibly smooth skin and the same sharp cheekbones as his daughter. He was also the warmest in his welcome, while the other Dr. Park, Kristin's mother, took on a more serving role. From what Kristin had told her, however, Sheryl knew that was not the usual way in the Park household. Kristin hadn't spilled that much about her parents—probably because of what Sheryl had told her about her own—but she had said that because her parents were both equally busy, they tried to divide all household chores evenly.

Kristin's father ushered her in, handed the bouquet of flowers Sheryl had brought to his wife, and escorted Sheryl straight onto the deck to admire his barbecue.

"Don't you think she's a beauty?" he asked.

"Don't mind him and his barbie," Kristin said. "It's his midlife crisis present to himself."

Sheryl didn't know much about barbecues, but perhaps Dr. Park was under the impression that she did. "Gorgeous," she said.

"Can I offer you some tea?" Kristin's mother asked, her voice high and tight.

"That would be lovely." Sheryl shot her a smile. It was strange to, at the same time, meet two brand new people to her, and be bombarded by features that reminded her of Kristin, the woman she had gotten to know very intimately in the past few weeks.

They huddled around the barbecue, as though it was a big treat to see the man of the house grill sausages. Kristin and her father drank wine, while Kristin's mother seemed to be greatly enjoying the tea she served. Sheryl stood in between them all, between the Parks, of which the older ones had magically produced the most divine child, a woman who made Sheryl's head spin every time she looked at her fine features, her slightly upturned nose, that pout in her lips.

When she'd first met her ex-girlfriend Andrea's parents, Sheryl had been convinced it would be awkward, that she wouldn't know how to behave, because she barely remembered what it was like to be in the same room with the two people who had made you out of their love—or, at the very least, a night of passion together. But when Andrea had taken her home and introduced her to her parents, all the awkwardness had slipped away, as though it had never even been there in the first place, and Sheryl had talked and talked, making up for all the family time she had lost—albeit with another person's parents.

It was the same that night. Sheryl struck up an easy conversation with Kristin's father, while her mother hurried in and out of the kitchen. Mid sentence, she would catch Kristin's eye, and notice how she stood there beaming. For both of them, in their own way, this was a big night.

"Can you keep an eye on these please, Sheryl?" Kristin's father offered her the instrument he'd been handling the meat with. "Please excuse me for a moment." With a graceful stride, he went inside.

"Christ," Sheryl said. "That man is very serious about his sausages."

"Everything rides on you not burning them," Kristin said. "If you do, it'll be West Side Story all over again."

They stood there snickering, while a warm glow unfurled in Sheryl's belly.

"They love me," Sheryl whispered.

"So do I," Kristin said, scooted a little closer and, just as her father came back out onto the terrace, planted a kiss on Sheryl's cheek.

Kristin flinched as she heard him and put some distance between them. All he did was shoot them a big smile as he slapped Sheryl on the back casually, and began inspecting the meat again.

———

"This salad is wonderful. Which dressing did you use?" Sheryl asked Kristin's mother.

While her mother rattled off all the ingredients—apple cider vinegar, sesame seeds, olive oil—Kristin tried to gauge the level of stress around the table. The person who seemed most relaxed was Sheryl, who had already explained in understandable language what exactly she was writing her doctorate's dissertation about.

While her father had been in his element when manning the barbecue, expecting Sheryl to be just as besotted with the equipment as he was, his jaw was now set and he chewed in a very controlled, tense manner.

But it didn't matter because Kristin was in the middle of an evening she had always believed would never come. She had brought her girlfriend home to meet her parents and no big dramas had transpired. Sure, there were some uncomfortable silences, which Sheryl always quickly filled, and her dad had gone a little overboard with the barbecue bonding, while her mother had played the part of zealous Korean housewife a little to the extreme as a way to hide her nerves, but it could only get better from then on.

Moreover, Kristin had the—perhaps silly—idea that she could give Sheryl a sense of family. That once her parents had gotten completely past the idea of their daughter being in a relationship with another woman, her parents' house, the home where she'd grown up in, could become a safe, homely haven for Sheryl as well; could give her something she'd missed since the age of twelve. Because, if anything, that's what Kristin wanted to give to Sheryl. A warm place to come home to. The sort of love she'd received from her parents: unconditional, regardless of expectations.

Kristin might have been nervous about coming out, about disappointing her parents and the dreams they might have had for her, but, deep down, she had always known that, even though it would make them uncomfortable and perhaps even sad for a while, they would still be there. As long as they lived, she would have their support, no matter who she was. A thought Kristin wouldn't have been so stupidly grateful for if she had been sitting at that dining table with anyone else but Sheryl, whose father was still alive but, from what Sheryl had told her, didn't care one bit who his daughter fell in love with. Even if Kristin's parents had openly disapproved of her relationship with Sheryl, Kristin would still have gotten more than the total indifference Sheryl received from her only surviving parent.

Kristin sipped from her wine, looked around the table again, and heaved a sigh of contentment.

"Would you believe I've never had kimchi before," Sheryl said. "How terribly un-worldly of me."

Kristin's mother shook her head and looked at Kristin, a small smile on her lips. "How dare you bring someone like that into our home," she said.

Kristin chuckled and heard her father utter a hint of laughter as well.

"Dad's just sad you can't put it on the barbecue," she said. "Though I'm sure he has tried."

Kristin found Sheryl's gaze and looked into her eyes, melting a little on the inside. Any other woman would not have had this effect on her parents, of that she was sure. Sheryl was charming them the way she had charmed Kristin. Just by being herself.

Sheryl shot her a quick wink, then refocused her attention on the conversation.

One phone call, Kristin thought, a few minutes alone with that smooth voice in her ears, had changed everything.

2007

CHAPTER ELEVEN

"But it's our anniversary," Sheryl said, trying to keep the annoyance out of her tone.

"I know. I'm so sorry, babe." Kristin didn't look very sorry to Sheryl. What she did look like was in need of a good night's sleep. But there she went again. Filling her suitcase with the same suits she always took with her on a business trip.

"Are you?" Sheryl was busy at work too, but no matter how many hours she worked, it always seemed to pale in comparison to Kristin's ambition and zeal to make it to CEO of Sterling Wines some day. If the promotion to Global Sales Manager she'd gotten a few months earlier was any indication of the future, Sheryl hoped, for Kristin's sake as well as her own, that that day would never come.

"What's going on?" Kristin took a break from packing. "You're not usually like this."

"It's our tenth anniversary, that's what's going on. That you even have to ask." Sheryl despised herself a little. This was not how she wanted things to be between them—and she didn't want to play this nagging part in their relationship —but she wasn't the one packing her bags again for the third time in the last two months. And while Kristin would be on her way to Bali or Sri Lanka or some other exotic destination, Sheryl would be home alone, left to the mercy of her demons, drinking a glass of fizzy water and watching TV to commemorate the day.

"This is work, babe. What can I say?"

It infuriated Sheryl when Kirstin used the work excuse,

as if it was the be-all and end-all. As if nothing, not even a ten-year anniversary, was more important than work.

"I guess that leaves me with nothing to say as well."

Kristin, though tired, still looked so well put together. "Here's a crazy idea. How about I use up some air miles and book an extra ticket. You can come with me."

"Go with you while you teach people all about how to drink."

They'd had the discussion on the ethics of Kristin's job before, and Sheryl really didn't want to go down that road again.

"You can lounge by the pool, read a bunch of books that you never get round to. Just relax." Kristin tried a smile —no doubt to try and derail the conversation from the route it was about to take.

"I can't just take time off."

"You could come for the weekend." Kristin took a step closer. "You could, if you really wanted to."

"You know I want to be with you, but not as a fifth wheel while you wine and dine hotel managers. If I'm going away with you, I want your undivided attention."

Kristin sighed. "You know how much this job means to me."

That shut Sheryl up, because she did know. It was impossible not to. In the past ten years, Kristin had worked her butt off to be where she was now.

"I can't help myself," she'd said to Sheryl in the beginning. "It's my Korean work ethic."

Sheryl had laughed at it then but had soon seen the truth in it because, it had to be said, all Kristin's parents ever did was work and whenever they visited, talk about work.

They had discussed at length the consequences of Kristin taking a job that would take her away from home for almost fifty percent of the time. They had, jointly or at least so it seemed, concluded that if it was the right career move, Kristin should accept the promotion. Not doing so would be career suicide. Kristin would either stagnate in her current position or have to start from a rung lower in another company. So it was unanimously decided that all promotions were good things, even though, and this baffled Sheryl most, Kristin's parents were doctors so they must notice the toll it took on their daughter's health. Though the outward signs of stress could easily be hidden underneath the excitement that comes with being offered a promotion.

Sheryl wasn't so sure of that joint decision any more now.

"Look, babe, I know this is a last-minute thing. And I truly am sorry about the timing, but I have to go. I have no choice."

Sheryl swallowed the question that had already made it to the tip of her tongue—"What would actually happen if you didn't go?"—and tried to shift her mindset into reconciliatory mode. She didn't want Kristin to leave in an atmosphere of reproach like this. Moreover, she didn't want to be this person whining for her partner to not go on a business trip. Kristin was right. Sheryl was not usually like this. Then again, she'd never needed to be before.

Kristin threw her arms around Sheryl's neck, and it still, always, sent a frisson of excitement down Sheryl's spine when she did. "Remember when it was the other way around?" Kristin said, her voice smooth as silk. "When we just met and you always had one meeting or another to attend in the evening?"

That was entirely different, Sheryl wanted to say. *I was fighting for our human rights, not selling alcohol all over the world.*

What bothered Sheryl most was that, despite having a long-term partner, she felt more alone now than before she and Kristin had met. She had always been busy then. Her life was filled to the brim with social activities, which had slowly dwindled away. Sheryl didn't have meetings with a bunch of like-minded women to look forward to anymore. She attended plenty of faculty activities, but in another capacity now: as Professor Johnson.

More than anything, Sheryl hated feeling alone, and that's exactly how Kristin's upgraded position at Sterling Wines made her feel.

Kristin put down her Blackberry for a few minutes. She hated missing their anniversary. She hated how her travel made Sheryl feel. So wasn't the conclusion obvious? Her Blackberry chimed—a noise that had started to make Sheryl flinch—but she ignored it. She'd have plenty of time to check her messages at the airport. Besides, she knew it was her boss asking the same question he'd been asking her for the past two weeks: have you made a decision yet?

She looked out of the taxi window. Night was falling. She had a seven-hour flight to look forward to. After taking the promotion almost a year ago, she had soon learned that business travel wasn't as glamorous as it was cracked up to be. Especially if your target market was Asia and you lived in Sydney. An issue her boss had pointed out not long ago and which had resulted in a subsequent question Kristin didn't know the answer to: would she be willing to relocate to Hong Kong? Settle there and have much easier access to the markets she was responsible for? Her flight times would be cut in half. It would be an adventure. It would be great for the company *and* for her career.

Kristin had been asked the question almost two weeks ago but hadn't brought it up to Sheryl yet. Before she did, she wanted to have a firm list of pros at the ready, along with a proposal of how all practicalities would be handled. She'd done some research on life as an expat and she was trying to put all of that together into a package to present to Sheryl, much like giving a presentation to a client. But, if she was really honest with herself, the real reason Kristin hadn't told Sheryl about this new opportunity yet, was because she knew that it wouldn't go down well.

She was afraid of Sheryl's reaction and of how it would

crush Kristin's dream immediately. Sheryl had only been a professor at the University of Sydney for three years. She had finally reached her destination after long years of work and doing all the crappy jobs professors didn't want to do. Kristin could simply not imagine Sheryl putting her career on hold for hers. Because it was always silently implied that what Sheryl did for a living was so much more important than what Kristin did—even though Kristin's job paid a hell of a lot more than Sheryl's.

Perhaps it was fitting for their relationship that they would spend their tenth anniversary apart. Kristin had heard of the seven-year itch, but she'd never heard of the ten-year one. She knew they were going through something serious enough for her to not be openly happy about being given another amazing opportunity at work. If she couldn't share that with her partner, no matter what they would decide to do, that was quite the itch. Kristin was afraid to tell Sheryl about the Hong Kong opportunity, and it said all there was to say about the current state of their relationship.

CHAPTER TWELVE

Sheryl desperately needed to get out of the house. She wasn't sure what would happen if she didn't. Well, she did, and it was that very thing she wanted to avoid. All this time she had to find a way of spending. So many people she knew were always going on about the luxury of time and how having time on your hands is just so great and blah blah blah. Time to be enjoyed with your loved ones, perhaps. Time to hang out with friends. Time to discuss the future. Time to learn a foreign language, to go for a hike, to unwind. Sure, that kind of time was more valuable than any money the jobs that ate away at time were worth. But the kind of time she faced then, the two hours before bed on nights when Kristin was away, seemed to open a void inside of her that could only be filled with one thing. The one thing that Sheryl despised the most, though despise was not the right word. She feared it, but she had also grown to crave it. And it was the very thing Kristin was away from home to promote.

Sheryl flicked through some channels. She should have accepted the dinner invitation at Aimee's, her former boss and now her colleague, but when she'd been invited, Sheryl had still been under the wrong impression she and Kristin would celebrate their anniversary together. It was a little late to call Aimee now. Perhaps she should go to a bar, on her own. Not in this neighbourhood, though, which was always teeming with students. She'd need to take a taxi. It was too much of a hassle. Sheryl didn't even want to go out, even though she didn't want to stay at home either. She couldn't decide. It was this exact sort of restlessness that drove her insane, that drove her to pace to the fridge and look at what it offered.

Sheryl pushed the door shut, applying pressure with her arms, as though it could possibly make a difference when she tried to open it again later. But this was the stage she hated. That sliver of time between still being fully present and giving in. Was this what it felt like to her father? Did he have to make daily, conscious decisions on whether he was choosing his daughter or the bottle? No, there was no excuse for what her father had done. Some days, Sheryl had to actively remind herself that he was still alive; that he, somehow, managed to take care of himself in a way that kept his heart beating. And for what?

She berated herself instantly for that question. But it was exactly to block out questions like this that very soon, within a few seconds, she already knew, she would remove her hands from the refrigerator door, open it, and take out a bottle of wine. She was the daughter of a woman who had committed suicide and a man who was a drunk. The depressive gene and the alcoholic one combined in one person, if such a thing existed. Hadn't she already proved enough? She would be forty soon. An age her mother had never reached. Hadn't she already beat all the odds? Research was a big part of Sheryl's job, yet there were certain things she couldn't even bring herself to look up online, not even after all these years. Could you inherit the inclination to become depressed? Did alcoholism run in families? She didn't want to know because she was afraid of the answer. Because it stared right back at her when she opened a bottle of wine, poured its contents into a glass. She didn't need scientific backup for that.

It wasn't as if she drank a lot. Just one or two glasses. Just enough to feel that mild buzz, to take the edge off everything she missed. Removing the cork from a bottle of wine had come to feel like a relief. Like the opposite of giving up.

It had started innocently enough, on a night when Kristin had been home. Kristin didn't have the habit of drinking at home, unless she was feeling really stressed. That day Sterling Wines had lost a client and Kristin felt responsible, the way she always did. She'd come home, walked straight to the fridge, and poured herself a big glass of wine. She'd drunk it quite swiftly, then poured herself another, and it was as though Sheryl could witness the change inside of her just by looking at her face. Her features relaxed, her shoulders unhunched, the tightness of her lips loosened into a small smile.

Sheryl had had a difficult conversation with one of her TAs, one she had misjudged and shouldn't have given the job in the first place, and she had not managed to circumvent all the usual reasons that stopped her from drinking. She just wanted her own lips to draw into a little smile. Wanted the tension to drain from her muscles just a bit. She wanted to experience what Kristin was experiencing. And while she had, it hadn't been a big aha moment. Sheryl had partaken in small amounts of alcohol before. She knew how it would make her feel, and it had been a conscious decision to seek out that very sensation at that very moment. She was in control. But then the arguments had begun and it had all been a matter of timing.

Their first fight about Kristin's schedule had mainly taken place inside Sheryl's head because she hadn't wanted to say all the things she felt roar inside of her out loud to Kristin. She wanted to be supportive. But by holding most of it in, and giving Kristin the impression that everything would work itself out, she had gone against her very nature. Or at least against her much-honed instinct of talking about everything until there was nothing left to say. She'd poured herself a glass of wine. But that first time of drinking on her own, it hadn't been relief washing over her. It had been a blend of guilt and euphoria, most of the guilt washing away as she drank more, making everything, not just how she felt about Kristin and her work situation, more bearable.

But before she drank, there was always a seal of tension to be broken. Because of her history. Because of how her father had ended up and how Sheryl had, from a young age, witnessed how it could destroy people. Then the rationalizing had begun. She wasn't a widow. She had Kristin, with whom she was, thus far, in a loving, committed relationship. She had her shit together. And it was only one glass—nothing compared to the amounts of strong liquor her father could put away in one sitting. Unlike her father, Sheryl was very much in control. And it wasn't as if she had any children who could lose respect for her because she had a glass of wine.

So there she stood—drinking was a standing activity— leaning against the kitchen counter. The cool wine made its way down her throat and almost immediately, a new sense of calm washed over her. Instead of an evening of agony over unresolved issues with her partner, the night transformed into one of possibility. Because the way a drink changed her perception about everything made all the difference.

Kristin had quirked up an eyebrow that time when Sheryl had drunk a full glass of wine with her. "Are you sure?" she had asked.

"It's just one glass," Sheryl said. After which Kristin had not asked any further questions. Looking back now, it had been so exemplary of how they'd been growing apart. A few promotions back, Kristin would not have just shrugged it off. She would have interrogated Sheryl about the reason she suddenly wanted a full glass of wine instead of the occasional half one at social gatherings. She would have taken an interest. But it seemed that Kristin's interest had shifted much more into the field of wine and how to sell it, and away from her partner.

Once Sheryl had finished the first glass, she caught her reflection in the oven window. She cracked a smile at herself, then shook her head. She knew the reason she poured herself the next drink, one she might even go sit outside on the deck with and savor, would be because of the question she had been trying to ignore: would she and Kristin be okay? Could they keep up with this new life that had come with Kristin's promotion? Was more money really worth it? Why did they need more money, anyway?

"It's a Korean thing," Kristin sometimes said, apparently unaware of how offensive that was to Koreans.

Sheryl had plenty more money than she'd ever had. She had Kristin. She had a great job and a bunch of nice friends. Maybe she needed a hobby, something to occupy herself with on lonely nights. Kristin had been right when she'd said that there used to be a time when Sheryl was always busy, always fighting for some cause, organizing fundraising parties while raising awareness to their plight. Activism was her hobby, and there was still so much to fight for. But most of her former pals had settled down, just the way she had done. They'd left the remaining battles for the new generation to fight. Besides, it wasn't as though Sheryl couldn't actually find things to do with her time if she wanted to. It was the fact that she didn't want to. She liked sitting around, thinking and talking, just laying it all out there, like they used to do.

Sheryl poured herself another glass of wine and walked outside. She looked at it, contemplating that she still had a choice: to drink or not to drink. As she slowly brought the glass to her mouth, she decided that, as soon as Kristin came back, they would have a real conversation about all the things that bothered her and where their relationship had gone. It was time to go into rescue mode.

CHAPTER THIRTEEN

"Hong Kong?" Sheryl was reacting in the exact way Kristin had predicted. "You must be joking."

"And you should calm down." Kristin could count the times she'd raised her voice in her life on the fingers of one hand. She was about to cross over to the second hand if Sheryl kept this up.

"No, you have to realize that I'm getting sick of playing second fiddle to your job."

"Sheryl, please, let's talk about this in a calm manner." Kristin almost said *like adults* but managed to keep that comment to herself.

Sheryl shook her head. "I can't believe you're even considering this." Sheryl was pacing up and down the room, her stride heavy, her face drawn. "So you can travel even more and I can sit around at home in a foreign country all day long." Sheryl stopped strutting around. "Don't you see we're already in so much trouble now?"

"It could be a new start." Kristin could try to make her arguments now, and she would, but she already knew Sheryl wouldn't be hearing them. "I asked around and there's a Gender Studies department at Hong Kong University. Things could be arranged."

"Things?" Sheryl stood with her hands on her waist.

"You could teach there. Imagine the difference you could make in people's lives." Truth be told, Kristin was going out on a limb here. After trying for a long time, she had finally managed to get someone from said department on the line, but the person's voice had been so demure and quiet, Kristin had not been able to understand much of what she'd said.

"It's not even about me being able to teach there. I don't want to teach anywhere else. I love it here. I've only been a professor for three years. I have ongoing research projects. Students who rely on me for their thesis. I have commitments."

"I just wanted you to know that this opportunity was offered to me. I've known for a while, but I didn't tell you because I could so easily predict this. Let's not discuss it for a few days while you mull things over. Talk to me when you're ready and when you've calmed down." Kristin briefly considered not adding the next part, but ignored her instinct. "But please keep in mind that this could be very lucrative for us."

Sheryl stood there, looking at Kristin for a while longer. Not for the first time, a sense of loss swept through Kristin. Like they were taking a step back in their relationship instead of forward. Would this proposition make or break them? Kristin recognized that they had, pretty rapidly, been reaching that breaking point. After ten years, and an anniversary spent apart, were they still going in the right direction?

Kristin watched Sheryl deflate in front of her. She sat down at the other edge of the sofa Kristin was perched on. "I just want you to choose *me* again. That's truly all I want."

Oh shit. Tears stung behind Kristin's eyes. Sheryl was always so strong, so boisterous. The way she sat there, all broken and ready to give up, made Kristin's stomach tie itself up in knots.

"I do. I do choose you." As she said the words, she knew they were a lie. She could have chosen to stay in Sydney for their anniversary, that would have been a start.

"Then where have all our good times gone?" Sheryl's voice broke. Would she cry? Kristin had never seen her cry. "Because if this is you choosing me, then I'm not sure it's enough."

"Oh, babe." Sheryl's bristling was so much easier to take than her breaking down. Had Kristin done this to her? Turned her into this woman who was about to lose all faith in their relationship? Kristin rose and sat next to Sheryl, throwing an arm around her. There used to be a time, not even that long ago, when they were always touching. Even when they went out to dinner, they would scoot their feet close together and bump their shins together, just as a little reminder of what they had between them. That whirlwind romance that had started ten years ago and had now turned into this. "I love you," Kristin said, as if it could solve everything. "I love you so, so much." Feeling the weight of Sheryl's body in her arms, her cheek pressing against her chest, reminded her of how much she loved Sheryl, how that love had grown and changed over the years, and how, perhaps, she'd let her ambition chip away at the beauty of it.

Kristin kissed Sheryl on the crown of her head. A couple of strands of hair had turned gray and she wondered if she was to blame for that too. Or perhaps graying hair ran in Sheryl's family, but if it did, neither of them knew.

She felt suddenly protective of Sheryl, of her pain— the one she'd lived with her entire life and the one Kristin had been causing her by being an absent partner. But hard work was all she had ever known. Kristin had been spoon-fed the sort of work ethic that didn't tolerate introspection. Both her parents had worked equally hard, while raising a child.

"I'm sorry," Kristin said before pressing another kiss to Sheryl's scalp. "For not being here." Sheryl didn't have many pictures of when she was a child, but Kristin suddenly saw an image, based on the few photos that had been rescued, of Sheryl home alone as a little girl, abandoned by everyone she held dear.

Maybe this was Sheryl opening up to her, reaching out. Showing a side of her that seldom surfaced. Kristin folded her arms around Sheryl a little tighter, hoping the fierceness of her embrace could say what she couldn't put into words. *I will never abandon you the way your parents did.* It wasn't that Kristin had lost the power of speech or couldn't find the words, but this subject was so unspoken between them, to broach it now might make Sheryl shut down, make her pull away that outstretched hand, close up the little crack she showed in that ever-strong facade of hers.

Kristin couldn't tell her in words, but she could show her with actions. Kristin felt a protectiveness toward Sheryl that was contrary to their relationship dynamic. Sheryl was always the strong one, so unflinching, so sure of everything she said and did. Sheryl wasn't the type to cry in Kristin's arms. Yet, there she sat.

———

Kristin probably thought Sheryl was crying because of the state of their relationship. While that certainly deserved its fair share of tears, the tears Sheryl was shedding, moistening Kristin's blouse in the process, were not solely born from grief over having to tell her partner she didn't want to move to Hong Kong, but because of what Sheryl feared it might do to her.

Kristin intensified her grip around Sheryl's body and Sheryl sunk deeper into her embrace. She knew where this was headed. She could so easily steer it away, divert Kristin's affection, but she didn't want to. Better an orgasm than a drink, she thought, and looked up at Kristin, knowing full well what the sight of her moistened eyes would do to her partner. She would see all sorts of things in them that she suspected Sheryl couldn't express—Sheryl knew this because Kristin had told her once.

"You don't have to tell me in words," Kristin had said. "I understand."

Sheryl had been both touched and aggravated by that. Touched by how Kristin tried, sometimes desperately, though always with a gentle, non-probing hand, to grasp

Sheryl's past, despite Sheryl's unwillingness to share much about it. What was done was done. Sheryl had already shared much more with Kristin than she had with anyone else. There really wasn't much more to say. What had annoyed her was the fact that this was the very reason she didn't talk about her mother's suicide with anyone. Sheryl wasn't after understanding because it bordered too close on pity, the very last thing she wanted.

"Come here," Kristin said, pulling her up, lips already parted for a kiss.

Kristin had been right about one thing. Sometimes, words were obsolete. They were in a bind, and this whole Hong Kong business had brought it to a head—something had to at some point. Just like Kristin had been unable to tell her about the offer, Sheryl was keeping her own secrets. If they couldn't be close by talking it all through, if too much stood in the way of that, they could at least express their willingness to understand the other through what they were about to do next.

They kissed, and it took longer than usual for Sheryl to shake off the tension in her limbs, the lingering hint of doom in her mind. But she knew Kristin's kiss so well, knew what the softness of her lips did to her, and how the familiarity of her touch made her go all warm inside. Kristin had always had a way of making her melt, a way of making Sheryl remember how things had been between them when they'd just met: passionate and so right from the get-go.

She pulled Kristin on top of her and melted more into their kiss, into the meeting of their bodies. Her mind relaxed and the tension in her muscles changed into an anticipatory one. Kristin trailed kisses along her neck, sank her teeth into Sheryl's shoulder, and, with that, set the tone for this particular encounter. Sheryl guessed this was makeup sex, or at least a diversion from all the conversations they had yet to have. Or, maybe, they *could* resolve it all without words. The whole notion of moving away from Sydney would dissipate as their orgasms roared through the air. Kristin would work less. Sheryl would drink less. She'd go back to abstaining again. She'd be strong again. She stopped her train of thought, realizing she was expecting way too much of a simple climax, while all Kristin had wanted to tell her, by quite roughly biting into her skin, was that she was ready and up for a quickie.

Sheryl tried to shuffle from underneath Kristin, which was a clumsy affair on the narrow living room sofa, to assume her more traditional position on top. But Kristin, uncharacteristically, wouldn't budge.

She used her teeth again and it made the hard pulse in Sheryl's clit intensify.

Kristin slid off her, pushed Sheryl's T-shirt up, exposing her braless breasts to the air. Then, unceremoniously, she flipped open Sheryl's jeans button and dug a hand straight inside her panties.

Just like during the course of a relationship all different kinds of love come to the fore at different times, the same was true for sex. But it had been a while since Kristin had done this, had taken control like this.

Sheryl reacted by lowering herself to meet Kristin's hand better. Kristin's slender digits never missed their effect, and just like she had allowed their embrace earlier to drain the tension from the room and her body, she sank into Kristin's touch there. Ready to go where Kristin wanted to take her at the flick of a finger.

Kristin's wrist didn't have much sway and Sheryl gave her a hand by lowering the zipper and pushing her jeans down a little. But, as it turned out, Kristin's hand didn't need a lot of leeway. She circled a finger around Sheryl's clit, gently, letting her get used to its presence there, allowing her body to catch up with the quick chain of events. As soon as Sheryl relaxed under her touch, she went from circling to rubbing. The rhythm revved up from slow to frenzied quickly, and Sheryl didn't stand a chance because after all this time together, Kristin knew exactly where to apply pressure. She didn't waste any time doing so and had Sheryl panting in a flash.

Sheryl marveled at the fact that Kristin could do this to her, could have her on the cusp of orgasm in a matter of minutes. Could undo the knots in her stomach and the worries in her head, at least for a little while.

The familiar heat spread underneath Sheryl's skin, swarming out, increasing underneath Kristin's finger.

Sheryl clasped her hands to the sides of Kristin's face and looked her straight in the eye. She gazed into Kristin's dark stare, met it head-on. The tiniest of smiles appeared on Kristin's lips. The kind that was so minute no one else but the person who knew her best in the world could see it, could decipher it for what it was. Sheryl latched on to it, then let go. She came at Kristin's finger with a strength that knocked her out briefly afterward. Then, when the shock had worn off, her hand still pressing against Kristin's cheeks, she pulled her close and, without words, told her how much she loved her.

CHAPTER FOURTEEN

Nothing had been resolved yet, and Kristin thought it important to show Sheryl she was making an effort. She had postponed her late-afternoon meeting until the next day and was on her way home to surprise Sheryl well before her usual time. They could order takeout and just sit on the deck and talk. Because they needed to talk more. Kristin was patiently waiting for Sheryl to broach the subject of Hong Kong, but it had been a week and she still hadn't said a word. Kristin didn't want to push her, but her boss was pushing her for an answer. If she said no—this had not been said in so many words at work but was silently understood—Kristin could lose her current position. The post of Global Sales Manager would go to someone else, someone willing to make the move to Hong Kong, because, of course, Sterling Wines wouldn't only be sending her there on an expensive expat package for her own convenience. The company was growing, their share in foreign markets kept expanding, and having a satellite office in a tax haven like Hong Kong made perfect business sense. If Kristin didn't go, someone else would.

But, she had decided, her relationship was more important than rushing Sheryl to make a decision. Deep down, she also suspected that no matter how long Sheryl pondered the question, the answer would always be no.

Before she turned the key in the lock, Kristin took a few deep breaths in order to push all work-related issues from her mind. She had come home early to improve their relationship, not to think about work.

"Babe, I'm home." Kristin did enough overtime to warrant her an early return home every Thursday, which was a day Sheryl often worked from home because she didn't have any classes or recurring faculty meetings. No reply came. Had Sheryl gone to the university today without telling her? Something must have popped up. For all Kristin knew, really, Sheryl could spend most of all Thursdays out of the house and she wouldn't notice.

Kristin saw a half-empty bottle of red wine on the kitchen counter, which struck her as odd. She walked over to it. It wasn't a brand Sterling Wines distributed. Did someone come to visit? Kristin looked out of the kitchen window and saw the back of Sheryl's head. Her heart sank at the prospect of them having company. That wasn't why she had come home early. Oh, well.

She headed outside to greet Sheryl and their impromptu guest, wondering whether Sheryl had many people over on Thursday afternoons. If she had, she'd certainly never told Kristin about it.

"Hey," she said, startled to only find Sheryl sitting outside, a glass of red wine in front of her.

Sheryl jumped. "What are you doing home?"

"Surprising you." Kristin took a step closer. "Looks like it worked." She eyed the glass of wine but didn't say anything.

Sheryl's glance skittered away. "You gave me a start."

"But you are happy to see me?" Kristin squeezed herself between the table and Sheryl's chair and sat down on her lap. "I thought we could talk a little." She smelled wine on her breath. She kissed Sheryl on the lips, then reached for the glass and took a sip. "Where did you get this? It's not one of mine."

"Someone at the university gave it to me. I, er, felt like trying it."

Kristin wrinkled up her nose. "It's not the best. Whoever gave this to you does not deserve full marks."

"Hm." Sheryl reached an arm around Kristin and pushed the glass away from them.

Kristin turned to look at Sheryl's face. Her lips were stained dark red from the wine. She had a light blush on her cheeks and her gaze was still skittering all over the place.

The question made it out of her mouth before she even had the chance to stop it. "Is there a special reason you're breaking out the wine in the middle of the afternoon?"

Sheryl shook her head. "Not really. I just thought I'd give it a try."

Kristin didn't inquire further. It was odd to find Sheryl like this, but so many things had been a bit off between them lately. "How about I get us a little snack to go with it then?"

"Sure." Sheryl smiled, pulled Kristin close to her, and kissed her neck. "Hurry."

Kristin went into the kitchen, sliced some bread from a fresh loaf Sheryl must have picked up earlier that day, and poured some olive oil into a small dish. When she gathered the crumbs in her hand and opened the bin to throw them away, she saw a crumpled-up supermarket receipt sticking to the top of the plastic bin liner. She automatically reached for it. The price of the loaf was listed on it, as was a piece of vintage cheddar, and a bottle of red wine. Kristin had to look twice to make sure she wasn't imagining things, but there it was, in black and white. The bottle of wine Sheryl had just claimed to have received from someone at work.

———

Sheryl felt trapped, caught red-handed, as though she had committed some sort of vile act, or worse, had been cheating on her partner, while all she had done was bought a bottle of wine and drunk from it. Kristin never came home early. Often, when she arrived back from a business trip around lunchtime, she would go straight to the office and put in a few more hours. This was unheard of. But Sheryl could hardly hold that against her. Not when she had just lied. And why had she? It had just seemed impossible to tell the truth. Sometimes, that was all a lie was. There was no bad intention behind it, just a complete and utter inability to own up to something that had grown into a weakness. It wasn't as if Kristin knew that Sheryl had bought the bottle herself, but that wasn't even the point. The point was that she had lied and no matter the reason or how easy it was to justify, Sheryl was not a liar. Not like that. Not to her partner. She would tell her the truth as soon as Kristin returned from the kitchen.

There she came already. A basket of bread in one hand, a small cheeseboard in the other. A tight smile on her face. As Kristin sat down, Sheryl tried to determine whether it was shame, that gut-wrenching emotion, that she was feeling the most. As a child, Sheryl had been no stranger to shame. It seemed to be abundantly available all around the house. Until, years later, she had said: no more.

"I bought the wine," Sheryl blurted out. "I can't really explain why, but I'll try if you insist." She said it to the space in front of her, the lawn that could do with a mowing and the weeds growing between the flowers. Kristin's mother would need to come around and tend to their small garden. It was one of her favorite Sunday morning activities—one that had kept Sheryl from taking responsibility for it.

"Are you okay, babe?" Kristin's voice sounded worried.

"I guess me sitting here with a glass of store-bought awful wine says it all." Sheryl turned to look at Kristin.

"What's going on?" Kristin touched her gently on the arm.

"I miss us." Saying those three words roused an unexpected bout of nostalgia from Sheryl's soul. She'd never before been under the influence when they'd had a fight. Well, this wasn't a fight yet, but the alcohol seemed to give Sheryl the ability to, oddly, see a few things a lot clearer, and she knew where this was headed. Another impossible confrontation between Kristin's ambition and Sheryl's loneliness.

"Me too."

"Then what are we going to do about it?" A feistiness she remembered from her activism days but never really played a part in her relationship with Kristin was coming to the surface. "This is as good a time as any to talk about the hard stuff, because what else are we going to do? Wait until it magically blows over?"

"This is about Hong Kong, isn't it?" Kristin withdrew her hand.

"Among other things."

"We'll need to make a decision soon." Kristin shuffled in her seat. "Have you thought about it?"

"I was just sitting here pondering it while drinking a glass of wine." The alcohol gave Sheryl the unexpected ability to control the anger she already felt boiling inside of her. Anger because she felt so blatantly disregarded, because the solution to the Hong Kong problem was so very simple —at least to her it was. Sheryl would never have guessed alcohol could do that to a person. It wasn't the kind of being-under-the-influence she remembered seeing as a child.

"I know you don't want to go." Kristin's words dripped with passive-aggression.

"Give me one good reason why I should give up everything here and move to another country? Just one."

"The reason is sitting right next to you."

"Nuh-uh. You don't get to do that. You don't get to use us, our relationship, our love, as a reason. It's not a reason. It's who we are. Or at least who we used to be. These days, I'm not so sure."

"If we don't go, I'll lose this job."

"And would that be so bad?" Sheryl blurted it out, and it felt damn good.

Kristin shook her head. "Thank goodness you've only drunk one glass. Or shall I pour you another so you can finally muster up the courage to tell me what you really think?"

"I've never lacked the courage."

"Oh no? Then why have we never properly talked about this? Only argued our way through a bunch of miserable fights that don't solve a thing."

"Because you see your job as some sort of holy grail that can't be criticized at all. Oh, it's work, so that ends every discussion, because of what work means to you. Like your self-esteem depends on it. Like there's nothing else more important than that company you work for. You sell wine. You're not exactly saving lives." Sheryl would not let this spiral into a critique on her personality so quickly. How could Kristin even think of accusing her of a lack of courage?

"And *you* do?"

"This has nothing to do with my job. My job does not interfere with our personal lives. When was the last time you came home from work and I wasn't here? I come home to an empty house every single day and I'm sick of it. I might as well live alone."

Kristin pushed her chair back a little. "Can't you see I'm doing this for us?"

"No, because you're not. I don't know why you believe work to be so important. Perhaps it's a sign of the times. Or perhaps it's because you feel you need to prove something to your parents. Perhaps you feel like making a lot of money will somehow tamper their disappointment about you not following in their footsteps and becoming a doctor. Perhaps it's even because you feel guilty about being a lesbian. The point is, I don't know why, but it sure as hell isn't for us. Because the only thing it's doing for us, is ruining us."

Kristin was silent for a long time. Sheryl's heart thudded violently in her chest. She needed another sip of wine just to calm herself down, but she was afraid to reach for the glass. Afraid of being judged for it. Afraid of needing it beyond a point of no return.

"So what do you suggest I do? Tell my boss Hong Kong is off the table, lose my promotion, take a pay cut and go back to my previous position?" Kristin said it as though she was suggesting someone chop off her right arm. As though the loss of title, prestige, and income equaled the loss of her inner strength.

"We can't go to Hong Kong and save this relationship at the same time. There's just no way."

"So you're asking me to take a step back for you."

"For *us*."

Kristin gave an almost imperceptible nod. "I'm not sure I can do that."

"I was afraid you'd say that."

"I'm going for a walk. A long one." Kristin rose. "Shall I pick you up another bottle of wine?"

Sheryl didn't say anything, just stared at the glass in front of her. She counted the seconds until Kristin left— after wanting to be near her so desperately all those times she was away, she just wanted her to leave as quickly as possible. Once she'd gone, Sheryl tipped the glass to her lips and drank.

CHAPTER FIFTEEN

Kristin walked and walked. She walked until Sheryl's words no longer reverberated throughout her. Until all she saw was Sheryl sitting on the patio with a glass of red wine in front of her. Had Kristin done that to her? Had she driven Sheryl to the bottle the way Sheryl's mother's suicide had driven her father to it? The image certainly shocked Kristin into giving herself a reality check. But why was it so hard for them? Cassie had two small children, ran a preschool, and had a successful marriage. Her boss Nigel, who worked about the same hours as Kristin did, had three children and a wife who worked part-time. She and Sheryl didn't have children, leaving them plenty more time to focus on work, so why was Sheryl freaking out about it so much?

While it was true that most of her colleagues were always complaining about lack of time, that was just the way it was. It came with having a high-powered job. Never enough hours in the day and a to-do list that stretched a couple of weeks. Stress. Not seeing loved ones enough. Up until recently, Kristin had never questioned any of these things. It was simply the way things were when you had a full-time job. Coming home from work and flipping open the laptop in front of the TV to catch up on e-mails. Setting the alarm half an hour early so she could arrive at the office before the others and catch up on some more e-mails before colleagues started to trickle in with their own needs and questions.

Had she been engrossed in work so badly she had ignored her own partner, who was now drinking in secret?

Which might not be a big deal for anyone else, but for Sheryl it was. No matter how lightly she brushed it off. It was a big deal. Because Kristin knew it wasn't just conviction and trauma that had been keeping Sheryl from hitting the bottle. It was fear most of all. Fear that she was more like her father than she wanted to be. Fear that she might see the dark side of him in herself when she looked in the mirror. Or worse, her mother's.

And yes, perhaps the solution to this problem was simple and Kristin should just take a step back at work. She was only forty. She had time to climb the ladder. Only, that went against every belief she'd ever held. Because Kristin worked harder than anyone else for a very good reason: she had no other choice. It was ingrained in her DNA. She didn't tolerate spelling mistakes in sales reports the way some of her colleagues did. She double-checked every single number she put into a spreadsheet. And it might take up more of her valuable time, but mistakes were simply not permitted.

She firmly believed that her attention to detail and her intolerance for mistakes had landed her that promotion. And now she would have to give it up? In what world was that fair? Because it didn't only mean her not doing the job anymore, but someone else, someone lesser, doing it.

Kristin rounded the corner again. She'd just been going around the block over and over. Every time she passed their front door, another opportunity presented itself to make up, to do the right thing. The only right thing there was to be done. Sure, she and Sheryl had had their problems over the course of their decade together, but they'd always, so easily, found a way out, and ended up the stronger for it. This felt different. Perhaps because it was so hard for Kristin to back down on this. But in the end, she always came back to that image of Sheryl and the wine. And their relationship. Their great, great love. Kristin started to realize that the reason she hadn't told Sheryl about Hong Kong straight away wasn't only because she was afraid of Sheryl's reaction. She had been afraid of what it would do to their relationship as well. She didn't even have to think about that anymore, because she had never really entertained it as a possibility. She imagined coming home from work every day in Hong Kong and finding Sheryl on the sofa with an empty bottle of wine. She'd give up a lot more to keep that from happening.

She'd have to talk with her boss, demand to be given another position in the company equal to the one she had now. After all, one of the main reasons Sterling Wines had thrived so much was because she worked there. Because she went to marketing seminars during weekends and on her own dime. Because she suggested they invest more in Asia. Because Kristin had only ever worked at one company in her life and she knew every single detail she was allowed to know —and a few she hierarchically didn't have access to.

She walked past their front door and went for another go around the block. She suddenly thought of the leaflet on time management her colleague Ted had left on her desk a few weeks ago. Kristin had cast a furtive glance at it and thrown it in the trash immediately. Who had time for nonsense like that? She was a perfectionist, but she still got things done quicker than most. She had the elusive quality of being able to combine speed with thoroughness. And she was paid handsomely to do it. She wouldn't take a pay cut. She couldn't. That would somehow feel like cutting into her own flesh. Not that money was what drove her most, but it was the number that most accurately reflected her work ethic.

Kristin approached the door again. She stopped and unlocked it.

———

"I'm worried about your drinking," Kristin said as soon as she walked in the door. Sheryl had retreated back inside. She'd poured the remainder of the bottle of wine away, assuaging some of her guilt as she watched it spill into the drain. She sat waiting for Kristin again, the way she would have done either way, even if Kirstin hadn't come home early to surprise her. And what a surprise it had been.

"I'm worried about it too," Sheryl admitted, out loud for the first time. "And I'm worried about us. The two might be related."

"We're not going to Hong Kong. I'll inform Nigel tomorrow. It was a ludicrous idea in the first place."

"It wasn't ludicrous, just not very realistic. It might have shortened your business travel times, but it wouldn't have changed anything for us. Besides, you wouldn't be able to see your parents every weekend. You'd be devastated."

"You mean they would be devastated."

"No, I meant exactly what I said." Sheryl rose from the sofa and went to stand next to Kristin, close enough to touch her if needed. "I don't want to stand in the way of your dreams, and if it really is your big dream to move to Hong Kong, then we can discuss it. But the terms you presented are not feasible."

"More than wanting to go to Hong Kong, I want to fix us," Kristin said. "I will tell Nigel I expect to be kept at a position similar to where I am now. He doesn't really have a choice, I've been an essential part of the company's growth and he won't want to lose me to a competitor. A minor financial loss might be inevitable, but I wouldn't be traveling as much. And things can go back to how they were before."

Sheryl was simultaneously impressed and worried. Kristin was actually putting their relationship first and she had managed to find a way to do so with only having to take a *minor financial loss*. But Sheryl worried that Kristin's unbridled ambition, that invisible thing that drove her to work her ass off for this company she didn't even own stock in or shared profit with, would never be fully satisfied. Maybe the kind of drive Kristin displayed could find a much better use if she started her own company. Not a new thought to Sheryl at all, but one she had never voiced out of fear that if Kristin were running her own business, she might actually work herself into an early grave. Perhaps the fact that she was paid a salary, which only went up at certain intervals, was what kept her from going totally crazy and working fourteen hours a day for a boss she only owed eight.

"Maybe we need some new ground rules," Sheryl offered. "Have a couple of date nights every week."

Kristin, who was leaning against the dining room table, said, "That sounds like a great idea."

"But you have to promise me one thing." Sheryl inched closer, curled her fingers around Kristin's wrists. "You won't hold not going to Hong Kong against me."

"I won't. I know it's not right for us." She slanted her head. "And who knows what tomorrow will bring?"

"Tomorrow will bring Friday and then Friday evening, when I will take you out for a nice date."

Kristin froze for an instant, the way she did, Sheryl knew from experience, when she was mentally checking her diary. "Can't wait," she said, after a beat, and stepped into Sheryl's embrace.

After a minute-long hug, which always managed to calm Sheryl down, Kristin whispered, "Now let's talk about you. Do I need to send you to AA?"

"I don't think that will be necessary," Sheryl said, injecting a confidence into her tone she didn't feel. "I'm hardly at the substance abuse stage, and the only thing I like about having a glass of wine is how it makes me feel for a brief moment."

"How *does* it make you feel?" Kristin took a step back and scanned Sheryl's face.

"Like everything will be all right."

"You don't need wine for that." Kristin kissed her on the cheek. "From now on, I'll be here to tell you."

2014

CHAPTER SIXTEEN

"I'm so, so tired," Kristin said, very aware she'd been saying the exact same thing every single evening for weeks upon coming home. It wasn't only a declaration of her mental and physical state, it was also a warning. A warning to the woman she loved: don't come too close, because I've had about all I can handle.

Sheryl looked up from the book she was reading, clapped it shut, and examined Kristin's face. "Straight to bed?" she asked.

"No." The only reason Kristin noticed the empty bottle of wine on the coffee table was because her foot bumped into it as she sat down next to Sheryl. "I want to sit here a bit with you."

"Do you want to talk about your day?" Sheryl asked.

Kristin shook her head. She just wanted to forget about this day that seemed to be never-ending. There used to be a time, not even so long ago, that she would arrive at the office early in the morning, and before she knew it, it was time to go home. The day would have just passed without her noticing, that was how engrossed she had been in work, dealing with one urgent thing after another, and never stopping to check the time, and, more often than not, forgetting to have lunch. That day had not been like that, nor had any others in the recent past. She'd butted heads with management again about which direction to take Sterling Wines into. A management she should have been part of by then, but wasn't because Sterling Wines had sold out to a big international group two years ago. Kristin's influence in most matters in which her opinion had always been respected and, more importantly, acted upon, seemed to have dwindled with every passing day.

"Do you want to talk about yours?" Kristin sank her head against Sheryl's shoulder.

"I had lunch with Martha. She finally came out to her children."

"Wow." Even though this was great news, Kristin found it hard to muster any enthusiasm for anyone's good tidings, not her own, few and far between as they had become, nor anyone else's.

"Shall we have her over for dinner some time?" Sheryl clasped her arm around Kristin's shoulder. Being ensconced in her partner's embrace worked like a temporary sleeping aid. Kristin could fall asleep there and then, but it would only result in more of the tossing and turning she'd been doing too much of in bed lately. "Babe?" Sheryl asked.

"Hm. Sure."

"I'll set it up," Sheryl said, and it was the last thing Kristin heard before she fell asleep on Sheryl's shoulder.

————

Sheryl couldn't move. Not if she didn't want to wake Kristin, who looked like she desperately needed every minute of sleep she could get. She listened to her partner's slowed breathing and took a deep breath herself. This was their life. Exhausted Friday evenings on the sofa, barely time for a decent chat. The bottle of wine Sheryl had easily polished off on her own hardly made a difference. She was of half a mind to open another, but that would involve moving and Kristin sleeping on her shoulder was about the pinnacle of intimacy they reached these days. Often, when Sheryl sat drinking alone, she wondered if this was it. If this was what it all amounted to. Despite not having to travel for work outside of Australia, Kristin's hours had still grown longer over time. Each year, she'd given that company a little bit more: more time, more dedication, more pieces of herself.

Parts of her that were once reserved for Sheryl had been squandered on work. But it wasn't what worried Sheryl most.

Kristin used to take such pride in her work. The sparkle in her eyes when she came home after a great day was almost worth not seeing her often enough. Because Sheryl knew what it was like to have a job that fulfilled you, an occupation that made it all worthwhile. But that sparkle had faded in the past year. These days, Kristin only seemed to give more and more, emptying herself into a void, without getting anything back. Her energy didn't get replenished anymore. She was depleting herself. Sheryl saw it. She suspected Kristin knew it. But she didn't know how to start that particular conversation, as if time had silently but slowly chipped away at their means of communication.

Kristin stirred, made a noise in the back of her throat, and pushed herself away from Sheryl. "I fell asleep again," she said, sounding apologetic, though this happened almost every night, and if she was truly sorry, she would perhaps try harder, however physically impossible, to stay awake.

"Don't I know it," Sheryl said, mustering a smile.

"Do you want to go to bed?" Kristen barely managed to suppress another yawn.

"You go. I'll be up in a bit." Every time she said those words—almost every evening of their life together, Sheryl mused: *the couple who goes to bed together, stays together.* They only went to bed together on weekends and, Sheryl had to be honest, then she was usually the one falling asleep like a log.

"Good night, hon." Kristin pressed a light kiss on Sheryl's cheek and went upstairs.

Sheryl looked at the empty bottle of wine. When was the last time Kristin had said anything about her drinking habits? Years ago. Then her mind wandered back to her conversation with her colleague Martha earlier that day.

"You and Kristin are my role models," she'd said. "I want what you ladies have."

"Be careful what you wish for," Sheryl had joked, put

on a smile, and hidden all the anguish, all the lonely days, and all the conversations they so desperately needed to have, behind it.

She got up and opened another bottle.

CHAPTER SEVENTEEN

Kristin looked at her corner office and the view behind it—one she wouldn't miss one bit. The surface of her desk was immaculate as always. She didn't understand how people could work in chaos. Whereas she had loved the gentle disarray of Sheryl's student flat when they'd first met, the coziness it created, her admiration had soon made way for stupefaction when she'd visited Sheryl's office. It had been such a big mess, Kristin's mouth had uncontrollably fallen open.

"You may not see it, but there's order in my chaos," Sheryl had said, her voice low and seductive, and Kristin had believed her. Kristin always believed Sheryl. Up until recently, she'd had no reason not to.

She walked behind her desk and sat in her chair. Would it be the last time? Did she owe it to herself to work through her notice period or just take gardening leave? After seventeen years, her best years, she certainly didn't owe it to the company. But she knew she would. She would train her successor, transfer her knowledge as best she could, and walk out of that very office four weeks from now guilt free. She'd not just given everything to Sterling Wines, she had given more than she had. Which was all well and good when she could thrive on the satisfaction she got from helping build the company from a local distributor to a worldwide one. But those times had long gone.

That morning, she hadn't come into work intending to quit. It had just been another dreary commute leading into a dreary, frustrating day. Until she realized, as she glanced over the number of e-mails in her inbox—most of them from her immediate boss—that she'd had enough. The joy she used to experience when working had slowly seeped out of her until every little thing had become a massive chore. It had taken a while, but that day, it really was as easy to sum up as that: Kristin had had enough.

She hadn't discussed her decision with Sheryl. She hadn't had time. It was a spur-of-the-moment kind of thing. A quick decision that would change the rest of her life—or at the very least her immediate future. No more ten-hour days. No more ten-minute lunch breaks in front of her computer, always catching up. She was done. Kristin suspected Sheryl would be pleased. She found her phone— that other torture device aside from her desktop computer at work and her laptop at home—and dialed Sheryl's number.

"Hey, babe," Sheryl said. Kristin heard chatter around her. "How's your day?" She sounded chirpy already.

"I quit," Kristin said.

Silence, then after a beat, "You what?"

"I quit my job, babe. I've had enough."

"Crikey." Sheryl was silent again for a few long seconds. "About time, I guess."

Kristin could barely make out what she said over the background noise. "Where are you?" It was the middle of the afternoon.

"The Flying Pig," Sheryl said. "I just popped off campus for a little breather."

Going by the noise, Kristin suspected it was a rowdy student pub. It wasn't hard to guess what Sheryl was doing there in the middle of the day. A fleeting thought passed through Kristin's mind: at least she didn't lie about it. As if that was something she should be happy about, something to cling to.

"When will you be home?" Kristin asked.

"When will *you* be home?" Sheryl countered.

"Five," Kristin said. "On the dot."

"I look forward to it already, baby."

Kristin hung up, scanned her office. As a place of hiding, it had served her well over the years. Now it was time to face the music.

———

"I had an extra drink in your honor," Sheryl said, her words so thick they were barely pronounced. "This is great news."

"I wish you'd waited for me to have that drink with." Kristin tried to put her annoyance aside. It wasn't Sheryl's habit to come home in a state like this, at least not as far as Kristin knew. She wanted to celebrate, not nag her partner.

"We'll have it now." Sheryl was already ambling to the fridge. "I think there's a bottle of champagne in there."

"How about I make us some food instead?" Kristin crossed the distance to the kitchen twice as fast as Sheryl. "We'll have that drink together another time."

"But… but, you quit your job. You're free, babe. We have to celebrate."

"You're drunk, Sheryl. It's five in the afternoon and you're absolutely hammered." Kristin turned her face away from the nauseating smell of Sheryl's breath.

Sheryl held up her hands, swaying. "I admit, I might be a little tipsy. That's all."

"Your definition of tipsy is very different from mine then." Kristin took a step closer to the fridge and leaned against it.

"I'm sorry." Sheryl seemed to deflate in front of Kristin's eyes. Fatigue washed over her face. Her limbs went soft. "I'm sorry." She sagged against a kitchen cabinet. "I truly am."

Kristin walked over to Sheryl and took her in her arms, her heart breaking a little. There could truly only be one reason for Sheryl's drinking. She must be suffering. And Kristin had been too busy to see it. Or no, she'd seen it, but she'd been too busy to do anything about it. To even talk to Sheryl about it. She'd figured Sheryl would correct herself along the way. She was a smart woman—she was a professor for crying out loud. But then, as they stood there in their kitchen, on the day Kristin quit her job and left her old life behind, she realized she should have done more. How else could a woman like Sheryl have strayed from her principles so much?

"We'll talk tomorrow," Kristin whispered in Sheryl's ear. "Everything will be all right."

CHAPTER EIGHTEEN

Sheryl woke with a start, like someone had pushed a button and flicked her brain wide awake. No sooner had she opened her eyes than her head began to throb in tune with her violent heartbeat. Slowly, she turned her head and looked at the alarm clock: 3:21. She turned her head to the other side. Kristin wasn't there. Instant paranoia took over. Sheryl sat up straight, causing a dizzy spell to rip through her. She racked her brain. Did Kristin have to go away for work? Wait. Had she really said she'd quit her job last night?

As dreadful as the moment of trying to scramble memories together was, it was nowhere near as excruciating as the one that followed. The one during which she was engulfed with shame. With the bitter taste of her own failure —once again.

Sheryl swung her legs out of bed and went in search of Kristin. She wasn't in the spare room, where she sometimes ended up when Sheryl snored too loudly. Sheryl headed downstairs and found Kristin asleep on the sofa, the TV still on.

She looked at Kristin as she stitched last night's memories together. The call at the bar. The walk home. Kristin's disappointment at the sight of her. The collapse in her arms. Nothing after that. Sheryl's tongue stuck to the roof of her mouth. The inside of her skull felt like someone was taking a jackhammer to it, adamant to make it through the thick bone. How had she ended up at The Flying Pig again? She had no idea. The reason usually disappeared. The reason for this embarrassment. For having her partner retreat to an uncomfortable sofa to sleep on. For that spark in Kristin's eyes to dim so swiftly at the sight of her.

Through the muddiness of her brain, and because she had no choice—because she always needed something to cling on to during those desperate moments in the middle of the night—the thought formed that things would be different now. Kristin had quit her job. Just like that. She hadn't even discussed it with Sheryl. The furthest they got in discussions about Kristin's job was how her ridiculous hours influenced their relationship, but Kristin was always careful not to promise something she couldn't deliver, not even in her personal life, hence she had never actually made Sheryl any promises. For a long time, guilt had eaten at Sheryl for not wanting to move to Hong Kong, for nipping that dream in the bud before it even had a chance to bloom, despite knowing, more than anything else, that it was the right thing to do for their relationship.

Things could truly be different from then on.

She pondered waking up Kristin and asking her to come to bed, but she figured she'd be better off with uninterrupted sleep.

She went into the kitchen and drank water straight from the faucet, eagerly gulping it up, and remembered an image of her father when she'd walked into the kitchen as a girl in the middle of the night. He'd stood there, his neck craned awkwardly toward the sink, trying to get as much water into his mouth as he could—trying to quench a thirst that would never go away.

———

For the past fifteen years, mornings had been a mad scramble to get out of the house. Sheryl could walk to the university from the house they'd bought ten years ago in Camperdown, whereas Kristin had to negotiate her way through early morning traffic in Sydney. Which, most of the time, meant that Kristin rose first and, by the time she was ready to leave, Sheryl's eyes only began to flutter open.

That morning was different, because Kristin had quit her job. Last night, after putting Sheryl to bed, she hadn't been able to sleep. Not only because of Sheryl's heavy breathing, but because of the decision she had made to just stop working. Her parents would never understand, though Kristin would tell them that weekend. She wasn't the type to keep secrets from them, not anymore.

She would still go into the office, but when she struck things off her to-do list, they would not be replaced by new tasks. She would be working toward the end. It was a strange sensation, a bit like taking her very last exams at university. Relief mixed with uncertainty. Whatever would come next?

Kristin had already polished off three cups of coffee by the time Sheryl came downstairs in an old robe that hung off her weary-looking limbs.

"Morning," Sheryl mumbled. Her facial expression resembled a puppy's who had been told off for an accident on the carpet. It was almost more than Kristin could bear. "You're still here."

"It's strictly nine to five for me from now on." Kristin rose from her chair at the kitchen table and slung her arms around Sheryl's neck. "How are you feeling?"

"My hair hurts." Sheryl cracked a tiny smile, showing a glimpse of the woman Kristin had fallen for so quickly years ago. "I'm sorry about last night. If I'd known…"

"We have all weekend to celebrate."

"The fact that your pending unemployment is cause for celebration really says it all." Sheryl curled her arms around Kristin's waist and pulled her close.

"I know." Kristin put her head on Sheryl's shoulder. "I should have discussed it with you before pulling the plug like that."

"I'm just glad you finally made the decision." Kristin tried to detect passive-aggression in Sheryl's tone, but she only heard fatigue.

They broke from their hug. Kristin poured Sheryl a cup

of coffee and they sat down for breakfast on a weekday morning for the first time in months.

"I could get used to this," Sheryl said and started buttering a slice of toast, then applied a thin layer of Vegemite. Kristin had been born and bred in Australia, but Vegemite had never been a staple in the Park house, and still, after all the years of living with Sheryl, the smell of it made her nose curl up in mild disgust.

"I'll still be going into the office for the next four weeks and do my job as usual," she said, "but I know all hell won't break loose if I don't get to the office before everyone else. It wasn't a huge epiphany, just a decision very long in the making. Sterling Wines hasn't been the same since it was bought up. It took me long enough to realize how unhappy the job was making me, but now that I have, I have zero regrets."

"So what's the plan?" Sheryl leaned back, cradling a refilled coffee mug in her hands. "The reinvention of Kristin Park?"

"I honestly have no idea." Not having a clue was a little scary. Her future a blank canvas. But it was also exciting and full of promise. "I've had enough of marketing for a while. I've had enough of corporations and overtime and younger colleagues whose sloppy work gets tolerated."

Sheryl scrunched her lips together before saying, "No more sexy business suits for you?"

"I can still wear them around the house if it makes you happy?"

"It doesn't matter what you wear around the house, babe, as long as you are *in* the house."

"How schmaltzy," Kristin said, even though she felt herself go a little warm on the inside.

Sheryl just shrugged and fixed her with a smile.

"I suppose I could become a domestic goddess," Kristin said.

"Who am I to object to that?" Sheryl sipped from her

coffee. "You can lick spoons like Nigella all day long. And keep making damn fine coffee like this."

Kristin chuckled. "Like this, you mean?" She picked up the teaspoon from the jam jar and slid the tip of her tongue up and down the handle.

"Have you seen Nigella do it?" Sheryl held out her hand. "It's more something like this." Slowly, she dragged her tongue over the hollow of the spoon, sucked it into her mouth and made it come out with a loud smack.

Kristin laughed, then said, "Koreans are more gentle spoon lickers, I guess."

They both broke out into more laughter. Then Kristin witnessed how Sheryl's face went serious again.

"I'm truly sorry about yesterday." She put her hand to her chest a little overdramatically. "I swear to you, I won't come home like that ever again."

"You had a bit too much. It's no big deal." Although it was a much bigger deal than Kristin was making of it, she didn't want to make Sheryl feel even worse than she already did.

"I don't go to the pub that much, but when I do go, time seems to slip away from me." A silence. "Do you remember how I used to be able to just have one glass?" Sheryl shook her head. "I seem to have lost that special ability entirely."

"You'll get it back." Kristin put her hand on Sheryl's.

"I don't want to be like him. It's the very last thing I want." Sheryl's voice was low but determined.

Kristin instinctively knew who Sheryl meant, even though they hadn't talked about her father in a very long time. "You're nothing like him at all."

CHAPTER NINETEEN

"I really should stop drinking," Sheryl said, as she poured herself and Kristin another glass of wine.

"Good start." Kristin picked up her glass. She had been away from Sterling Wines long enough to not automatically think about her former job anymore every time she had a drink.

"You know what I mean." Sheryl just stared at her glass.

"Not really." After so many years together, Kristin guessed they had both picked up the habit of assuming they always knew what the other meant without having to spell it out. Perhaps on some level, this did happen, but Kristin failed to truly comprehend what Sheryl meant. Because she never pushed when it came to Sheryl drinking too much. It was an uncomfortable area to venture into, a topic so entangled with memories and scars, Kristin didn't even know where to begin.

"I don't want to become an alcoholic," Sheryl said. Always the same phrase. Like a statement, a declaration of intent. Except the words were so hollow they didn't mean anything to Kristin. Possibly because Sheryl only spoke them when she'd already had too much.

"You are not and will never become an alcoholic." Kristin sipped from her wine, on the verge of feeling guilty for enjoying its aroma. Sheryl had a way of spoiling the pleasure she took in the very moderate amount of alcohol she consumed.

Sheryl had worked from home and Kristin hadn't been

able to figure out what to do with herself all day, aimlessly wandering through the house and tidying up every stray object she came across. She'd been without a job for a month, and it was beginning to make her restless. Kristin had never been without a job or clear purpose before.

"I think I'm well on the way." Sheryl didn't let up.

Kristin had a choice. She could let Sheryl go through her usual spiel and endure five more minutes of her feeling sorry for herself for being the alcoholic she wasn't really, or do the thing she never did: call her out on it. Sheryl had spent more time outside of her home office than in, and annoyed Kristin every time she ventured into the living room, unwashed in a scraggly T-shirt she'd owned since they had met.

"I really wish you would stop saying that." Some of the irritation she'd amassed over the course of the day had seeped into Kristin's tone of voice.

Sheryl quirked up her eyebrows. "Someone's a bit snippy." With that, she tipped the glass of wine to her lips and took a large gulp.

I'm not snippy, Kristin thought, *I'm aimless*. She made a point of not taking it out further on Sheryl. This, however, didn't mean they shouldn't have the conversation they never had. "I know you have this strange notion that one day you will turn into a drunk because your father was one—"

"*Is* one," Sheryl corrected.

Kristin went on, unperturbed. "I understand it makes you wary, makes you feel a little guilty even, every time you have a drink. But it doesn't make you an alcoholic. Alcoholics are addicts and you are not an addict, babe."

Sheryl sighed that particular sigh that usually indicated she was about done with a topic. As though what she really needed to assuage the guilt and shame that came with having a drink, was to acknowledge her fear out loud.

"I just... feel like it influences my life more than it should. And that, over the years, I've started to drink more and more. I used to not drink at all, then just one glass when we were out with friends, and look at me now. Drinking on the patio with you. Going to The Flying Pig in the middle of the afternoon. Opening a bottle when I'm home alone. I feel like it's escalating and there's nothing I can do about it."

Kristin sat up a little straighter. "If it bothers you so much, then maybe you should try stopping, or at least drinking less. You know you have my full support."

"That's just the thing." Another sigh. "The thought of doing so scares the shit out of me."

"Why?"

"Because it's hard. Because alcohol is everywhere. Because a beer after a long day at work is about the most divine thing there is." She shrugged. "So many reasons."

"You didn't drink for the longest time, remember? Why would it be so different now?"

"Because I feel like I crossed a line that can't be uncrossed. Once I started drinking more, I realized how that very first sip, and the comfort of a near-full glass in front of me, made me feel so much more alive and at ease and full of possibility. In that respect, I do feel like I'm an addict. So much so that I've begun to understand my father, the man who let me down so much. I get it. And as it turns out, I'm not like you. I can't just have two or three and stop. My ability to do so is out of the window after that first glass."

"It didn't used to be. You used to be so disciplined."

Sheryl shook her head. "Back then, it had nothing to do with discipline. It was a mere matter of principle. I might have had a glass in front of me, but it was just for show, just to not feel like a pariah in this booze-crazed country where not drinking makes you look like a spoilsport or an uptight judgmental bitch. I didn't really know how it made me feel because I didn't give myself the opportunity. I only felt disgust for this substance that took away whatever was left of my youth after I had already lost most of it."

Kristin didn't know what to say to that, so she put a

hand on Sheryl's knee and squeezed. "How about this," she said. "How about you follow my lead. If stopping altogether is too hard, why don't you let me curb your intake? Only drink when we're together and I'll let you know when it's time to stop. You can count on me for that."

"How do you do it? How do you know when it's time to stop?" Desperation clung to Sheryl's words. This time she really did appear serious. Or perhaps all the previous times, Kristin had been too preoccupied with other things to listen.

"Because I can't help but think about the consequences of one more glass and the prospect of a hangover is more than compelling enough to make me stop."

"I suppose we can give it a try." Sheryl covered Kristin's hand in hers. "But enough about me. What are we going to do about you?"

"I wasn't aware something needed to be done about me." Kristin tried to sound shocked, but she knew exactly what Sheryl was talking about.

"You're not someone who does well without a proper occupation." Sheryl squeezed her hand. "Either you get yourself a very time-consuming hobby or you start looking for a new job."

"Maybe I should become an adult student of Gender Studies. Go to all your classes," Kristin joked.

"You're very welcome to come to any of my classes, just don't expect preferential treatment."

"I wouldn't dream of it." Kristin raised both their hands and planted a kiss on Sheryl's knuckle. "Speaking of fun pastimes, when are we going to that shop we've been talking about in Darlinghurst?" Kristin waggled her eyebrows.

Sheryl fixed her with a stare. "Very, very soon," she said.

———

Sheryl opened her eyes, then abruptly closed them again. It felt as though if she even so much as blinked, all the memories from last night came rushing back, whereas when she kept her eyes tightly shut, she could keep a lid on them. But no, even the darkness could no longer hold back the resurgence of the words that had fallen from her mouth last night—because that was the only way she could describe it. She hadn't consciously *spoken* the words. That thought would make everything even more unbearable than it already was.

There was the memory, crystal clear in her mind: Kristin's father had insisted on having a barbecue, the way he always did when Sheryl came over. Somehow, over the years, it had become a way for them to bond—as if the thought that Sheryl was the 'male figure' in the relationship she had with his daughter made him feel more comfortable. The one who 'manned' the grill with him while Kristin and her mother made salads in the kitchen. While this sort of stereotypical thinking went against everything Sheryl believed—and taught in her classes—she had allowed him to get away with it from the start.

"Lecturing them will make things very uncomfortable," Kristin had said.

"Speaking the truth has a tendency to do so," Sheryl had replied. "It doesn't mean you should lie."

But it had been the beginning of their affair and Sheryl wanted Kristin's parents to like her and, really, if that was what it took, this tiny transgression, then yes, she would allow Kristin to convince her it was all for the better, to keep the peace and not ruffle anymore feathers.

After they'd eaten, and Sheryl had ignored Kristin's subtle cues that four beers were enough, and as Kristin's father cleaned up the barbecue, she had let him pour her some of that rice wine he always talked about, but Sheryl never felt compelled to taste. Surprisingly she had liked it. With the ingestion of it, an extra dose of verbal confidence, which was not something Sheryl lacked even when sober, had seemed to come over her. Looking back, it had been a bout of foolishness, but at the time, it had felt like the polar opposite.

"I guess your wife is kind of my mother now as well. And you're kind of like my surrogate dad," Sheryl had said, and it had felt so good and so true to her, that she had nodded approvingly at her own comment, completely ignoring Kristin's father's reaction.

But it didn't matter how he had reacted. It didn't even matter that she could have said much worse—something along the embarrassing lines of what a fine-looking woman his wife was. Looking back on that short bout of conversation, in the cold light of day, the only conclusion was that she shouldn't have said it. It was not how the Parks conversed with each other. Way too much intimacy was conveyed in that stupid little sentence of which Sheryl didn't even know the provenance. It was just utterly ridiculous. But a disturbing thing had happened.

When Kristin started putting a well-meaning hand on her knee and didn't top up her glass the way she did with the others', Sheryl had brushed her off with a simple flick of the wrist because she was convinced she wasn't drunk. She felt a mild buzz, but it didn't impair her in any way and it didn't spiral into the boozy madness the way it used to. Instead, she was convinced that the copious amounts she'd put away didn't affect her one bit. And went on to blurt out silly things like likening her not-even-legal parents-in-law to the parents she'd lost a long time ago, even though one of them was still alive.

The shame she used to feel just for drinking too much was now multiplied by sheer mortification at embarrassing herself in front of Kristin's father.

Because of this, her headache felt worse, her limbs felt heavier, and she didn't want to get up at all. But she had promised Kristin they would finally, after weeks of saying they would but never getting round to it, go to Darlinghurst, to that shop and all it stood for in their relationship. She couldn't possibly blow Kristin off because she had a heinous hangover, not after ignoring her obvious signals to stop drinking the night before, and violating the unspoken code they had drawn up between them.

CHAPTER TWENTY

"Can we turn the music down, please?" Sheryl asked. She groaned when Kristin lowered the volume. Sheryl had spent most of the ride yawning and sighing. Now it looked like her headache had intensified since they'd left home on their shopping venture. Kristin gladly ignored the signs of Sheryl's massive hangover. She had done her very best to stop this hangover from happening at all, but as had quickly become the custom, Sheryl had again ignored her gentle prods to switch to water after a couple of drinks. Clearly the plan Kristin had come up with to curb Sheryl's drinking wasn't working, and the fact that she was even trying to was having an adverse effect on their relationship.

Instead of her usual spiel of profusely apologizing for drinking too much and saying inappropriate things, Sheryl was also saying sorry for ignoring Kristin. It wasn't so much the fact that Sheryl had ignored her—because, really, that was to be expected of an inebriated woman with a strong will of her own—but all the endless apologizing she felt she had to do the day after.

Kristin was fairly sure Sheryl saw this entire trip to Darlinghurst as a way of atoning, because she sure as hell didn't look in the mood for sex toy shopping. It was hardly the right atmosphere for a little excursion that was meant to inject some much-needed vitality back into their intimate life. This was supposed to be fun. They should be giggling like girls half their age—not that Sheryl was the type to giggle in a sex shop.

"This place has changed," Kristin said, after she had

struggled to find a parking spot.

"Gentrification," Sheryl said in between groans.

Over the years, they had become very confined to their set neighborhoods. They had bought a house in Camperdown, close to the university, and Kristin worked in the Central Business District. Most of their friends, who were mainly people Sheryl knew from the university, lived in the same area. And somehow, Kristin had forgotten there was a whole city outside of their cramped circle. A city with up-and-coming neighborhoods like this one.

The street they'd parked in was residential with neat rows of houses with a cozy deck at the front. When they arrived on the main road, bustling with Saturday afternoon activity, they stopped at a real estate agent's window.

"Bloody hell," Sheryl said. "Can't wait for Camperdown to gentrify. Our house will be worth a fortune."

"When did we come here last?" Kristin asked. "This place is unrecognizable." Kristin scanned the other side of the street. There was a coffee shop, the obligatory yoga studio, a juice bar, all squeezed in between restaurants offering the most exotic cuisines.

"I don't know if we ever even came here. This was always too sleazy for you, babe." Apparently Sheryl's hangover had receded enough to give her back the ability to joke.

Just walking down the main street, examining the menus and inhaling the electric atmosphere, Kristin found a new bounce in her step. She'd been cooped up in the house and her own neighborhood and habits for too long. She already knew she'd be back in this area, to see what it was like on an ordinary weekday. She had all the time in the world to explore.

"You do know what gentrification equals, right?" Sheryl hooked an arm through Kristin's. "Breeders and strollers." Her voice dripped with cynicism.

Just as she said it, they had to make way for a mother

pushing a toddler in a state-of-the art stroller. After a few more steps, they encountered a man with a baby strapped to his back.

"Oh yes." Sheryl nodded vigorously. "They have arrived already."

"But will they have already driven out the gays?" Kristin chuckled. "Or are they coexisting peacefully?"

"Peace is still upon us." Sheryl tipped a finger to her forehead, the way she always did when she assumed she was crossing paths with a fellow lesbian, a habit that drove Kristin crazy with its presumptuousness as much as with its whiff of elitism.

"How is it elitism?" Sheryl had asked when Kristin had called her out on it once. "How can you even consider that word for such a suppressed subculture as ours?"

"Because it excludes others."

"So?" Sheryl had stroked her chin the way she did when she was about to go into professorial mode.

"How do you even know if someone is gay, anyway?"

"I knew when I saw you." That had put an uncontrollable smile on Kristin's face.

"Where is this shop?" Sheryl asked. "It looks like it doesn't belong in this neighborhood anymore."

"Let me check my phone." Kristin looked on Google Maps. "It's probably on the other side of that big intersection over there."

"How about a hipster coffee first?" Sheryl said, looking very much like she needed a giant dose of caffeine.

"Crikey," Sheryl said. "I always forget how much money there is to be made selling coffee." They were sitting by the window, waiting for their drinks.

"It's at least a dollar more per cup than anywhere near the uni. About the same price as in the CBD." Kristin was not an accountant by education or trade, but she had always found a lot of joy in making the marketing budget, despite marketing dollars spent not always being quantifiable when it came to results. She always came up with a way, usually by means of a complicated calculation, to put a more precise price tag on the strategies she pitched.

"When you really think about it, it's utterly ridiculous to pay four dollars for this." Sheryl pointed at the steaming mug in front of her.

"But clearly not ridiculous enough to stop us, and many others, from doing so."

"Remember when we first met and we went on our coffee date? How much did we pay for a cup then?" Sheryl shook her head. "I'm on the verge of feeling severely ripped off."

"I don't feel ripped off at all. You pay for more than the coffee. You pay for the experience and the service."

Sheryl cocked her head. "Does your coffee have a substance in it that mine doesn't?" She gave a small smile.

"No, but I guess my body is in a better state to receive it." Kristin didn't pay much attention to Sheryl's reaction to her jibe. The germ of an idea had been planted somewhere deep in her mind.

"It *is* good coffee," was all Sheryl said.

Kristin looked around. The coffee shop was small but cozy. She thought about a discussion she'd had years ago with someone working in the marketing department of Starbucks, who were trying to gain ground in Australia.

"Ozzies love their coffee," he had said, "and they're willing to pay for it, only not to us." Since hearing that, she'd paid notice every time a new Starbucks branch popped up somewhere, and how it was almost always mainly visited by tourists. When it came to coffee shops, Australians really did have a fiercely independent streak. And they truly couldn't get enough of it, what with the way coffeehouses had sprung up everywhere in the past decade.

Kristin had spent a large portion of her career making foreign markets fall in love with Australian wine. Could she possibly make Australians fall in love with American coffee? No, joining another marketing department didn't make her heart beat faster, especially not one of a big international chain, no matter how challenging and possibly rewarding it might be. What really made her heart beat faster was a place like this.

"On the way over to the shop, I'd like to stop by that real estate agent again. Just to have another look."

"Sure." Sheryl knocked back the last of her coffee. "But first I'll have one more overpriced cup of this."

When Kristin was mulling something over, she turned inward. Sheryl could strip naked right there in the street and Kristin would hardly notice. Her brain was churning, Sheryl could tell. What she couldn't tell, was the subject occupying Kristin's mind so much she suddenly seemed to have lost interest in visiting the sex shop that had been the very reason for their trip to this neighborhood.

They were walking in the direction of the shop regardless. It made Sheryl think of the long and heated discussions she used to have with her fellow grad students and LAUS members on the importance versus the insignificance of sex toys. A bout of nostalgia rushed through her. Last she'd checked—and it had been a while—LAUS membership had gone down again. Did that mean that lesbians nowadays missed out on the conversations she used to have? Or was it all a matter of context and general inclusion, and they just talked about all of it openly with their straight friends, no distinctions made or necessary? How the world had changed.

When they finally found the shop, tucked away in a tiny alley, its facade so discreet you really had to know what you were looking for, Sheryl remembered the reason Kristin had insisted they'd come.

During one of her cleaning-up sprees, of which she'd had many since becoming unemployed, she had found the dildos and harnesses they used to fuck each other with, and had been appalled by the state of them.

"It's silicone," Sheryl had said. "Just pop them in the dishwasher and they'll be good as new."

Kristin had stood there with her hands on her hips. "There's no way I'm using these *ever* again. They've become unusable by not using them." She'd wrinkled up her nose.

Sheryl had quickly sussed out the real reason for Kristin's indignation and agreed to go shopping for a set of new ones.

Sheryl hadn't entered a sex shop in a decade. The products on offer seemed to have multiplied.

This, however, didn't seem to deter Kristin at all. She went straight for the display in the back, Sheryl following her, picked out two that looked almost exactly the same as the ones she had binned a few weeks prior, cast a furtive glance at the vibrators, seemed to decide against them, and —as though time had suddenly become of the essence— without consulting Sheryl very much at all, headed to the register.

When they stood outside, Sheryl grabbed her by the hand and asked, "Why the sudden hurry?"

"Something has come up," Kristin said. "We need to talk."

CHAPTER TWENTY-ONE

"You're probably going to think I'm crazy," Kristin said.

"There's also a good chance I won't," Sheryl replied.

"Wait until you've heard what I have to say." They were drinking coffee in the living room, the plastic bag with the toys they'd bought discarded somewhere in the kitchen.

"I'm all ears." Sheryl sank back onto the sofa. She looked a million times better than this morning, when Kristin had practically had to drag her out of bed.

"I had this idea and now I can't stop thinking about it."

"So I've noticed." Sheryl sported a hint of smile.

"I need something to do. Something I can be passionate about. Something of my own."

"I'm in triple agreement."

"How about opening a coffee shop?"

Sheryl's eyes grew wide. She sat up a bit straighter.

Kristin didn't give her a chance to counter-argue. "You said so yourself earlier. There's money to be made with coffee."

Sheryl leaned forward and put her elbows on her knees.

"Obviously I haven't yet thought this through. I haven't done any of the math. I'll need a business plan."

"You'll need much more than a business plan."

Kristin shook her head. "No. It's all I need, along with the support of my partner."

"You always have my support." Sheryl looked at the carpet when she said it.

"I can't go on moping around the house all day doing nothing. I don't much feel like joining the corporate world again. And today, as we sat there in that coffee shop, in that amazingly vibrant neighborhood, the thought came to me. And why not? What have I got to lose?"

"Apart from a bunch of money?" Sheryl looked up.

"Money is just money. We have plenty of it in the bank. Enough for me not to have to work for another five years at least. What if I did something else with it?"

"I did see a twinkle in your eye."

"It was more than a twinkle, babe. It was an epiphany."

"Looks like you'll have to pitch me the idea then. Once you have it all worked out on paper."

"You know I will. You know you won't be able to resist my finely honed pitching skills and wizardry with numbers. You're basically a lost cause already."

"Don't just pitch me the business behind it. I'm more interested in the lifestyle that comes with it. I don't think either one of us wants you to go back to working the insane hours you did for almost twenty years."

"That's the beauty of being your own boss: hiring employees."

Sheryl's face didn't look immediately dismissive.

"Just dream with me here for a second. A place of our own, decorated exactly how we want it, making a couple of dollars margin on every cup of coffee we sell."

"Hiring young and nimble baristas," Sheryl joked.

Kristin gave Sheryl a look, then remembered what had brought up this line of conversation in the first place. The toys they had bought, now forgotten in the kitchen—the last place they should be.

She looked at Sheryl again, with different eyes this time. The fresh air, the walk, and the coffee must have done her a world of good, because she looked like herself again, as opposed to the pale, stiff-limbed woman Kristin had roused from bed that morning. She looked like the woman Kristin had wanted to drag to that sex shop. A glint in her eyes. The shadows under them all but evaporated, and what was left of them lending her a slightly dangerous edge. One Kristin hadn't taken advantage of in a long time.

"How about we take our new purchases upstairs?" Kristin regretted not having taken more time to explore in the shop, but her mind had been so preoccupied all of a sudden, as though the thoughts she was having couldn't possibly wait, not for the fifteen minutes more they could have spent in the shop, nor for the closer-to-five that they actually did. "I'm sorry for being so distracted earlier." It was important to apologize because Kristin knew that this was what she did: she lost herself in projects. Working twelve-hour days was never an issue for her as long as she completely believed in what she was doing.

The thought of opening a coffee shop—and a thought was really all it was at this point, perhaps a silly one, but perhaps also a viable one—injected a different kind of energy into Kristin's veins. One she wanted to share with her partner.

"I know what you're like when you've got your eye on something." Sheryl said, a half-cocked smile on her face. A smile Kristin recognized so easily.

"I was focused on the wrong thing at the wrong time. My bad." Kristin slanted her head, hoping that the look in her eyes conveyed exactly what she really wanted to say.

Sheryl's eyes narrowed as they fixed on her. "Go upstairs," was all Sheryl said.

Kristin obeyed.

———

Sheryl took her sweet time unwrapping her new toy, cleaning it, and getting ready to join Kristin in the bedroom. This was her favorite time of the day. Her hangover had worn off and she felt at ease enough with everything, herself, her relationship, her life, her memories, to not feel that itch for a glass of wine yet. But, as she stepped into the panties that came with the dildo, and mused about their ease of use and the difference with the more old-fashioned straps she used to fasten around her hips and always got caught somewhere they shouldn't, she also felt her age.

When she and Kristin had first bought strap-on dildos, the whole endeavor had been a wild adventure. From scouting where to buy it, to ending up in the most sleazy, women-unfriendly shop, and bringing the purchases home all giggly and excited, unable to keep their eyes and hands off each other for a single second.

Everything was different now. They had both changed. Their bodies and their personalities had, over the years, done a subtle shift from always ready to a more sedate state. And, as she stood there in the bathroom, avoiding the sight of herself in the mirror, then berating herself for doing so, Sheryl wondered if she had aged well. Kristin was right when she'd said their toys hadn't been used in years, and Sheryl asked herself if her body would still be up for this. She hadn't taken care of herself the way Kristin had, though she knew it was futile to compare.

Sheryl shook her head, stepped in front of the full-length mirror and tried to admire herself. The sight of this used to excite her so much. This game they were about to play used to have her jumping out of her skin with anticipation. Whereas then, she felt more like she was getting ready for a performance.

It wasn't so much that desire had slipped away with her youth, because Sheryl felt plenty of desire at many different times, but her relationship with her own body and with Kristin had changed. Sheryl could derive the utmost pleasure from watching Kristin rise in the morning, sitting on the edge of the bed, stretching her still-taut body before tiptoeing into the bathroom. She took great comfort in pressing her breasts against Kristin's warm back before falling asleep at night, an arm slung protectively over her body, pulling her in as much as she could. But that was companionship. A different kind of intimacy requiring a different kind of mindset than the one needed for what they were about to do next.

When Sheryl walked into the bedroom, she found Kristin kneeling in front of the bed, her torso resting on the sheets, her head turned away from the door. She didn't stir, didn't give any indication she had heard Sheryl walk in, though she must have. She was playing her part.

The atmosphere in the room was serious and quiet, like the calm before a storm. Sheryl slapped the other toy, the one she'd had to dig deep into a drawer for to find, against the palm of her hand. Just the action, paired with the sensation of the leather slapping against her hand, made her perk up. Made her step into that much-needed mindset.

Sheryl caressed Kristin's ass cheeks with the back of her hand, ever so gently, just to state her presence, and to contrast with what she was about to do next.

Without any further ceremony, she thwacked the paddle hard against Kristin's right butt cheek, then her left.

Kristin's body shifted with the impact, but she didn't make a sound. Sheryl saw her nails dig into the sheets, though, a sight that didn't fail to arouse her.

Sheryl let the paddle come down again, a little lighter this time, but only to fool Kristin, by no means to give her any respite. The next round of strikes was so hard and merciless Sheryl felt the blowback reverberate in her muscles. She brought her free hand between Kristin's legs and found her as aroused as her cheeks were colored pink. Her lips were swollen and wet. Sheryl dragged a finger along her opening and smeared the wetness onto the dildo.

"You're so wet," she growled. "So horny and wet." She could feel her own wetness moisten the panties she was wearing.

At this, Kristin did groan, and Sheryl couldn't wait to see her tear-stained face. Kristin could sometimes be so stoic, so composed and in need of control of every single process in her body, and it took all of Sheryl's willpower to continue until the tears came.

Sheryl blasted another round of blows on her ass, then slowed her pace. She let long, silent seconds go by before landing another hit, and listened carefully in between for signs of Kristin's distress. Nothing.

She delved her fingers deeper in between Kristin's folds, sensing her increasing wetness, and again, transported the moisture to her toy—not that she would need that much of it later. Kristin was already soaking wet.

It had been a long time since they'd done this, and while Sheryl was surprised how easily she'd found her groove again, that dominant streak that flourished in situations like this, she had to do her best to remember the boundaries they'd once set.

Kristin could take the pain. She relished it. That part hadn't changed. But Sheryl was more worried about what she could say. She used to spout the nastiest language, calling Kristin much fouler things than the requisite *bad girl*. It seemed a good place to start for now.

"You've been a bad girl," she hummed, but the words felt wrong as they tumbled from her lips. Kristin was pushing fifty, she was hardly a girl. Despite it being part of the fantasy they had once created, that part of it didn't seem to work for Sheryl anymore. She believed she was still in tune enough with her partner to know that merely calling her a bad girl wouldn't influence her level of arousal at all, perhaps even take away from it.

Sheryl folded her body over Kristin, making sure she could feel the heft of the dildo against her inner thigh, and half-whispered, "You've been a filthy slut again, haven't you?" She waited a beat for Kristin's reaction, which came in a low-pitched moan, confirming that Sheryl was on the right track. "I'll fuck the sluttiness right out of you."

A rush of lust sped up her spine as she pulled back. She let the tip of the dildo slide into Kristin's pussy a tiny bit, and retreated, before starting on another round of controlled but ruthless spanking. How easy, she thought, as the paddle rained blows on Kristin's ever-reddening butt cheeks, for us to pick this up again where we left it years ago. And in that thought, she concluded, lay the essence of their happiness. Their success as a couple. Because they might not do this every week or every month—or even once a year— anymore, but they would always have it to return to. This intimacy that was uniquely theirs, the products of their personalities and proclivities and, as a result, something that could never be recreated with anyone else. This was them— at their best and most sleazy.

Sheryl threw the paddle on the bed, and it was the first time Kristin raised her head. Sheryl realized she should have just let it fall to the floor to maximize the effect of the dildo brusquely breaching the rim of her pussy, and burrowing deep inside from the get-go.

Sheryl thrust deep, and even though it was the dildo sinking inside of Kristin, not any direct part of her own anatomy, it felt like coming home after a long, exhausting journey. She put her hands on Kristin's blemished behind— the paddle would leave its mark for a few days—and lost herself in the motion, in the intoxicating sensation of claiming Kristin in this way. She couldn't see her face, yet she felt more connected to her than she had in a long time.

Sheryl put everything else out of her mind, everything that had built up since the last time they'd done this—with the old set of sex toys. As though the purchases they had made held much more than just hygienic value; they held a symbolic one as well. New toys, new ideas, renewed intimacy.

The thought Sheryl had had when standing in front of the mirror earlier came full circle. Yes, she—they—had changed. The rapport between them had changed, had grown deeper in some areas and more flimsy in others. But no matter what—no matter her flaws, or Kristin's—they had this between them. They had love. A past and a future. And an exquisite present.

"Oh," Kristin moaned.

Sheryl allowed Kristin to push herself up a little by lowering the intensity of her thrusts. As if she'd only seen Kristin do it yesterday instead of too long ago, she predicted her partner's next move. She caught Sheryl's deep strokes on one arm and brought the other one between her legs to touch her clit.

She was close. Sheryl knew what to do. She changed her pace to a controlled, steady thrust and, with her right hand, slapped Kristin's ass on the exact spot where a deep red blush had formed.

Kristin groaned harder. Her hips bucked wildly. Sheryl let her hand come down again. Hard enough to tip Kristin over the edge, but not too hard to leave any more marks. Sheryl had left enough of those already.

Kristin let out a prolonged, syncopated half yell, then collapsed onto the bed. The dildo slipped out of her, and as Sheryl stepped out of the panties as swiftly as she could, she noticed her legs were trembling. This had taken more out of her than she remembered it doing, but it didn't matter. What mattered was the sight of Kristin, crawling onto the bed to have her full weight supported—her knees must be sore and marked as well—her ass cheeks striped red, her body language projecting utter satisfaction.

Sheryl composed herself and flanked Kristin on the bed. "Do you like our new toys?" she asked, her voice hoarse.

It was the first time she got a good look at Kristin's face and she found it wet with tears. Kristin nodded. "Though my brain is muddled by an unbelievable climax, I can see everything so clearly." She huddled up a little closer to Sheryl. "I'm going to open a coffee shop," she whispered. Her words barely audible. "We're going to do it together."

CHAPTER TWENTY-TWO

They had moved fast. After that first walk in Darlinghurst, Kristin had gone back several times in the following weeks and contacted all the real estate agents in the area. Perhaps she'd been as lucky as Pat, the agent, had told her she'd been, though Kristin suspected that much of her proclaimed luck was really sales talk. They'd found a perfect space only a few weeks after Kristin had laid out all her plans to Sheryl, including the suggestion to sell the house and move to a different neighborhood.

Sheryl had been living near the university her entire adult life, from when she was a first-year student at the tender age of eighteen. Kristin knew it would be a hard sell, but her enthusiasm and the utter suitability of the property for their purposes had quickly won her over.

Sheryl would have to commute to work from then on, and she wouldn't be able to pop home in between classes when she needed a break from colleagues and students at the university. But Kristin hadn't even needed that much power of persuasion.

"You battled traffic for almost twenty years," Sheryl had said. "Now it's my turn. And I'll get a damn good cup of coffee to help me through."

Kristin had been surprised by how easy it had been to convince Sheryl of all the changes she proposed. Starting a business from scratch, moving to a new neighborhood, living in an apartment above the coffee shop instead of their house.

"I stood in the way of your dream once before," Sheryl

had said. "I have no intention of keeping this one from coming true for you."

When they'd had that conversation, Kristin had seen all the reasons she'd fallen in love with Sheryl shine through so clearly. Her convictions, her confidence, her trust in Kristin.

"For all we know, if you hadn't stopped my burning ambitions then, we wouldn't be here now," Kristin said. At the time, giving up on moving to Hong Kong had been a bitter pill to swallow, but in hindsight, it had been the best decision. Perhaps not for her career, but most certainly for her relationship and her life in general.

Now they stood in their very own coffee shop: The Pink Bean. Kristin had thought long and hard about the opening party. Daytime or evening? Alcohol or coffee only? For the longest time, she had leaned toward coffee only, out of consideration for Sheryl, until she realized it wouldn't be consideration at all, just a means of controlling her alcohol intake.

Almost every other time they sat down for a glass of wine, Sheryl still proclaimed she ought to stop drinking, but she never did. Right then, she stood with an empty glass of champagne in her hand, talking to one of their new neighbors, who had all received an invite for the opening.

The woman Sheryl was talking to had long curly auburn hair and the clearest green eyes. From where Kristin was standing, it could have looked like Sheryl was flirting with her, though Kristin was sure she was only imagining that and was more worried about where that sudden bout of insecurity had come from.

She shook hands with a few people, exchanged pleasantries, and accepted congratulations as she headed over to Sheryl and the woman she was talking to.

Sheryl and the neighbor both stopped talking as Kristin approached.

"The woman of the hour," Sheryl said after a beat. "Amber, this is my partner Kristin, who made all of this happen. Honey, Amber teaches yoga just around the corner and is so persuasive I almost signed up for a trial."

"Nice to meet you, Amber." Kristin shook her hand, while, subconsciously, putting her other hand on Sheryl's shoulder.

"This place is halfway between my apartment and the studio where I teach, so I guess you'll be seeing more of me. Provided you also sell tea."

"We most certainly do." Kristin held Amber's gaze. "And I look forward to serving it to you on a daily basis."

"Don't let her bully you into too much patronage," Sheryl said. "She's a crafty marketeer."

"I look forward to it too," Amber said. "Sheryl told me you're new to the neighborhood, so welcome. I like that you're so open about everything as well, by the way. Some people might argue that we don't need more of that, but I think we do."

Kristin was probably the only one who noticed the subtle shift in Sheryl's stance. She rooted herself a bit more firmly to the ground and her shoulders squared a bit more solidly, as though guessing correctly at someone's sexual preference gave her cause to grow a little taller.

Kristin herself had only pegged Amber as a lesbian because of the way her head had inclined when Sheryl was talking to her. Sheryl still had that instant effect on women. Sadly, Kristin felt she had grown mostly unaware of it after so many years together.

"It's *extremely* important," Sheryl stated.

With glee running up her spine, Kristin concluded that Amber would soon learn all about the ways Sheryl thought it was important to be out and proud. Kristin knew her arguments by heart, though they had changed and become more nuanced over the years.

"There's still so much to fight for," Kristin heard Sheryl say, pecked her on the cheek, feeling a little thrill at the reawakening of the activist in Sheryl, and went to greet a couple that had just arrived.

If the turnout at the opening was anything to go by, The Pink Bean would be a great success.

What Kristin didn't realize, was how in awe Sheryl was of her. Probably because she didn't tell her enough, though Kristin seemed to have made a point, even through the most hectic stages of the renovations, of having enough time for them as a couple. On paper The Pink Bean was owned by both of them, but in reality, all of it, including the design-in-progress of their apartment upstairs, was all Kristin's doing. Sure, they had discussed everything, but all Sheryl ever had to do was say yes or no to something Kristin brought to the table. She mostly said yes. And this was what her saying yes all those times had amounted to. A brand-new business, a brand-new life for Kristin, for whom being busy and working toward something was the pinnacle of happiness. She was the kind of person who needed something like this.

How exactly Kristin had pulled this all off in a matter of months, Sheryl wasn't entirely sure, despite being witness to it all. She tried to be as involved as she could be, but The Pink Bean was Kristin's baby and what Kristin needed most of all was her unwavering support, not her opinion on which tiles to use in the bathrooms. The only aspect of the entire endeavor they had discussed in depth was the name. Sheryl had been the one to suggest it, not only because Darlinghurst was a very gay-friendly neighborhood, but because she thought it important to state who they were from the get-go, rainbow sticker on the door and everything.

Of course Sheryl had had her fair share of doubts. How could she not have? But she was due for a change as well. Kristin quitting her job had been the catalyst for all of this, for their reinvention as business owners, though Sheryl would just continue working at the university the way she always had. Secretly, she hoped the change in daily routine and environment would spark a more personal transformation as well—thank goodness Kristin hadn't set her sights on opening a pub, because that might well have been the end of her.

"Hello, stranger." Caitlin sidled up to her. "Who would ever have thought? You and Kristin owning a coffee shop?" Sheryl had invited her old friend on a whim, and to her surprise, she had been in the country and shown up. She was probably on the prowl. Maybe she should introduce her to that woman she and Kristin had just met, the yoga teacher, who had made Sheryl's gaydar buzz all over the place.

"Perhaps it was always in the cards for us," Sheryl mused. "But we never truly know, do we?"

"You've become even more philosophical in your old age," Caitlin said. "Every inch the wise professor I knew you would one day be."

Sheryl bumped an elbow into Caitlin's arm. "I'm forty-five. You can call me wise but old is pushing it a bit."

"Don't you love it, though? Being in your forties?" Caitlin said in the same conspiratorial tone she'd always talked in. A tone that made Sheryl realize how much she'd missed her friend. "When you're finally beginning to realize what truly matters in life."

Sheryl glanced at Caitlin. "And what are your findings on the subject?"

"I, for one, couldn't give one more flying fuck about what anyone thinks of me and my ways."

Sheryl chuckled. "As far as I can remember, you never cared about that in the first place."

Caitlin shook her head. "I cared a little, which was still too much." Sheryl noticed how Caitlin's glance stuck to Amber. "All that matters is being true to yourself." She took a swig from her champagne glass. "Now tell me, old friend, do you have any way of introducing me to that cute ginger over there, or am I going at this cold and alone?"

"I've got your back, sister," Sheryl said, as a throwback to their early university days. "All you have to do is ask."

Sheryl introduced Caitlin to Amber. Earlier, Amber had listened attentively to her little speech about visibility and all the ways in which it matters, her green eyes lighting up a bit, the way they used to, years ago, in girls who had just joined LAUS. Sheryl wondered what Amber's story was, and she marveled in the fact that, because of this coffee shop she owned with her partner, she would soon be able to find out.

Sheryl looked around. People were chattering away, some meeting each other for the first time—like Caitlin and Amber—and some who had been neighbors for a while. Already, a sense of community was in the air. She had to hand it to Kristin once again: she knew an opportunity when she saw one, but more than that, she knew how to seize it when it presented itself.

She found Kristin in the thickening crowd and looked at her for an instant while a waiter refilled her champagne glass. As the level of bubbly liquid rose in her glass, so did the amount of respect and love she had for her partner who had pulled this off.

2016

CHAPTER TWENTY-THREE

Sheryl was going over the results of a research study two of her grad students had conducted. She often found herself coming down to work in the cozy, bustling atmosphere of The Pink Bean rather than in her office upstairs. She loved the hum of conversation around her and the sense of being surrounded by people more than the quiet of her study. What she loved most, though, was being able to watch Kristin from the corner of her eye.

Kristin had worked hard the past two years, often pulling week-long twelve-hour daily shifts behind the counter, because she was the sort of perfectionist who had trouble delegating even simple tasks like handing customers their change. These days, she employed a couple of people to do the work with her—one of them, Josephine, a student of Sheryl's. A shy girl who Sheryl had pushed to take a job in a busy coffee shop when she'd asked her if she knew of any job openings. Sheryl was certain Josephine had meant a job at the university, but she'd also been sure that the girl would benefit more from a job that would put her into direct contact with a bunch of strangers. And she had. At least as far as Sheryl could tell. She made a mental note to check in with Josephine at the end of her shift.

Sheryl refocused her attention on her laptop screen and was just starting to recognize a pattern she'd been hoping to find, when the door opened. A man walked in and Sheryl did a double-take. He sort of looked like her father, but also sort of didn't.

Instinctively, she rose. First, she looked around for

Kristin, who had never actually met him, but she was in the back or upstairs.

Her father spotted her and walked up to her, hesitation in his steps. How did he recognize her so easily after all these years? His beard was neatly trimmed and his eyes were strangely clear. As he approached, Sheryl realized she was looking at an old but sober man. That was why she'd barely recognized him. He didn't match the memory she had of him.

"Sheryl," he said, his voice matter-of-fact. "Can we talk?" He didn't make any moves to kiss or hug her, which Sheryl appreciated. They had lost contact decades ago. Though never a deliberate choice on Sheryl's part—she couldn't be sure of her father's inebriated intentions—it had happened and it had been a relief. Because all her father reminded her of was the atrocity of her mother's death. It was all he embodied for her because of what he had allowed it to do to him. And Sheryl soon realized there was no saving grace in hanging around a man who liked drinking more than spending time with his only daughter. Not if she wanted to save herself.

Sheryl gave him another once-over. He wore a jean jacket and trousers, a bright white T-shirt underneath. The stark cleanliness of the outfit struck her. Clean clothes was another thing she'd forgotten to associate with her father— the person who was supposed to do her laundry after her mother had died. He was skinny as a rake. Despite looking sober, he didn't look very healthy, with his pale, yellow skin and sunken eyes.

"Do you want some coffee?" Sheryl asked.

"Just some water would be great, thanks." Her father sat down without being invited to.

As she went to fetch a bottle of water and some glasses, she took a few deep breaths—Amber had been telling her about the immediate effect they can have on your psyche.

"Look at you," he said, after Sheryl had sat down opposite him and clasped her laptop shut. "All grown up."

"I'm forty-seven," she said. "I've been grown up for thirty years." Before Sheryl and Kristin had bought their house, she had received the odd birthday card at her apartment, back when her father still had an address for her.

"I know. I know," he said. "I'll be seventy in a couple of weeks."

Every year on her father's birthday, Sheryl contemplated getting in touch. In theory, it wasn't hard to do. He probably still had the same phone number, because why would an alcoholic bother to change numbers? And if not, all Sheryl had to do was go down to Campbelltown and ask around. But every passing year when Sheryl made the choice to cut him out of her heart and her life a little bit more, the distance between them lengthened. Despite being dressed in jeans, he looked more like a man in his mid-eighties than approaching seventy.

"I've been doing the twelve-step program," he said, his eyes flitting from here to there. "Successfully, this time."

"Don't tell me you've come to make amends." Sheryl didn't know how else to be than on the defensive. Her heart was not made of stone and she even felt sorry for her father, who had lost most of his own life as well on the day he found his wife hanging from a rafter in the attic.

"I know I can't ask forgiveness of you, but I do need to tell you how sorry I am." He shuffled in his seat. "My liver is not going to hold out much longer. It has been failing for a while now, something I can't blame it for." He gave a mild, derisive chuckle.

"Oh." Sheryl wished she had a glass of wine standing in front of her instead of water.

"I didn't mean to barge in on you like this and deliver all this news, but I don't know how else to tell you. I thought about writing you a letter, but... but I guess I just wanted to see your face. Look you in the eye."

"How long have you got?" The tremor in Sheryl's voice surprised her.

"Not long," was all he said.

"I'm sorry." Maybe it was because she saw her own eyes reflected back at her, only much more weary and bloodshot, but Sheryl truly was sorry. She had always imagined a phone call from the police, telling her matter-of-factly that her father had been found dead. While she was glad that it would never have to come to that, having him sit in front of her and give her the news himself was just as harrowing.

"When did you find out?" Sheryl asked.

He cleared his throat. "I've known something was up for a long time, but I've only been sober for four and a half months and going to a doctor was hardly a priority when I was still on the sauce."

"And you still decided to stop drinking?" Though she barely knew the man, it seemed so unlike him.

"It's never too late." That mirthless chuckle again.

Sheryl didn't know if he was joking. She had no way of telling. It had been too long. Too much time and life had passed between them. Inside her, a war waged between seeing herself in this man and all the distorted, mostly unpleasant memories she had of him. All the times he had let her down. At first, when she came home from school, she'd find him on the sofa, sleeping it off. But soon after he lost his job, he spent most of his time in the pub down the road, and Sheryl spent most of her time at her aunt's. Though Sheryl always felt she needed to stay to take care of her dad, and to tackle the bottomless grief they'd been plunged into together. Who else could possibly understand what it was like to lose her mother like that? To be deserted by the person who gave birth to you?

"Looks like it is," Sheryl murmured, hoping his hearing was failing as well.

"I know I've been the worst kind of father and I also

know I don't deserve to know any of the things I would like to know before I go, but I would like to learn about your life. About you."

Sheryl cocked up her eyebrows. "Excuse me if I think it's a little late for *that*."

He leaned back in his chair. "Oh, it is surely too late for that. I'm well aware. I missed everything. Drank it all away. I don't blame you for your reaction. I don't blame you for a single thing. But I had to come see you and ask. I had to."

Sheryl didn't know what to make of all of this. This sudden appearance. She and Kristin were happy. They had this place. Sheryl had her career. They had good friends and a good relationship with Kristin's parents. Sure—and this was the thought that stung the most—Sheryl was a bit loose-handed when it came to pouring wine, but she didn't have any big complaints about her life. Everything was going great. And now her father had turned up. She'd put the anguish her parents caused her behind her decades ago. At least she thought she had. She hadn't counted on her father materializing like that—all apologetic and sober.

When she was still a teenager, she had often fantasized about him sobering up, but had never detected any signs that he ever would. Thus, her father had lodged himself into her mind, and then her memory, as the pathetic drunk he was. Soon, she didn't even feel sorry for him anymore. Because who was there to feel sorry for her? No one. She was only a young girl and she *had* gotten her shit together. She had found a way to recover from the unspeakable tragedy of her mother's suicide. Her father hadn't. It had taken him thirty-five years to pull himself together.

"All I ask is that you think about it." He started pushing his chair back. "I just want to talk. Get to know you a little." Was that a tear glistening in the corner of his eye? "Let me know." He fumbled in his pocket and put a small piece of paper with a couple of digits scribbled on it on the table. "That's the number of the place I'm staying. I don't have a mobile phone, I'm afraid."

Sheryl looked at the piece of paper. She imagined him writing down his number, his fingers trembling as he hoped for the best. Why was it so hard to give him a clear no? She wanted to, felt she needed to in order not to burst a huge delicate bubble inside of her, but she couldn't.

She palmed the piece of paper and said, "I'll think about it."

———

Kristin heard Sheryl come up the stairs. She was about to make a phone call but waited so she could ask how things were going downstairs. Living above The Pink Bean was great in many ways—a very short commute, being the main one—but it did fail to put any kind of distance between her and what was now her job.

"You look pale as a sheet, babe," Kristin said. "Did Josephine set something on fire?"

"I just talked to my father," Sheryl said, and steadied herself against the fridge.

From the very beginning of their relationship, Sheryl's father had always been an elusive figure. Ever since Sheryl opened up to her for the first time in the cabin in the mountains, Kristin had pledged never to push her on the subject. She figured that Sheryl would start the conversation if she wanted to have it. She never had an issue doing that when it concerned any other topic. But Sheryl never did talk about her father, and Kristin had continued not to push.

"Wh—How?" Kristin walked over to her. "Did he call?"

"He was here. I sat with him at a table downstairs." Sheryl's voice was shaking.

"What did he say?" Kristin didn't know whether to put her hands on Sheryl's shoulders or not. Whether to draw her into a hug and try to make the sheer shock displayed on her face go away.

"He's sober." Sheryl shook her head. "And dying,

apparently. Nothing like death tapping on your shoulder to make you see the error of your ways, I guess." Sheryl's voice trembled with years—decades—of pent-up hurt and disappointment.

"Let's sit down for a bit." Kristin gently took her by the hand and walked her to the living room.

"I need something," Sheryl said after she'd sat down. "Something strong."

Kristin knew what she meant, didn't hesitate, and fixed them both a whiskey, adding lots of ice, because it was the middle of the day.

"I think I might be in shock," Sheryl said, tipped the tumbler to her lips and drank it all in one go, the ice clattering idly against the glass. "Never in a million years…" Her voice trailed off and she stared ahead of her.

"What did he want?"

Sheryl sighed. "To get to know me before he dies." She turned to look at Kristin, and Kristin couldn't remember a time she'd seen so much helplessness cross her partner's face.

"Fuck." Kristin didn't swear often, but this occasion called for it.

"He gave me his number." Sheryl fished a flimsy piece of paper out of her jeans pocket. "And I don't know whether to tear this up or frame it and hang it on the wall." She huffed out a disdainful breath. "What am I supposed to do with that?"

Sheryl's eyes pleaded, as though searching Kristin's face for an answer.

"What did you say to him?" Kristin wished she had been there.

"He asked me to think about it and I said I would." Sheryl looked around, got up, and found the bottle of whiskey on the kitchen counter.

"Will you?" Kristin tried to keep her tone as gentle and light as possible.

Sheryl refilled her glass in which the ice had not had time to melt, then cupped it between her hands—as though she could draw strength and a clear head from doing so. "I have no choice but to think about him now." She sighed. "All these years. It's not that I never thought about him anymore. Of course I did. It's not even that I didn't understand his reaction after Mom died. But I wished so hard for him to pull himself together for such a long time, and when he never did, I had to let him go. Had to push thoughts of him away as soon as they popped up. It was hard enough having one parent desert…" Her voice caught and she sipped from her whiskey, more carefully this time. "As far as I'm concerned, he left me too. They both did. And we never, ever talked about it. About why she did it. Not even on the rare occasions when he was sober." She went silent.

"He probably just wants to know you're doing okay."

Sheryl shrugged violently. "Maybe. But we don't have a relationship, despite sharing DNA. I don't know the man, and I don't feel he has the right to know me. Not anymore."

Sheryl drank more, finished her glass; Kristin had barely touched hers. Then she let her head fall into her hands. Kristin caressed her back, squeezed her shoulder, listening for sounds of her crying, but didn't hear anything.

"I could have gone the rest of my life without thinking about him. Now he has given me no choice," Sheryl said as her face reemerged.

Kristin sidled up to her, put her arm more firmly around Sheryl's shoulders. "Maybe it can be a good thing. Maybe you can get some closure." The barely broached subject of Sheryl's family always threw up a certain distance between them. Because Kristin didn't know that much about them, only the bare minimum facts. Maybe she should have pushed more in all the years they'd been together, perhaps even taken advantage of Sheryl's more frequent bouts of drunkenness.

"I always believed I already had closure." Sheryl put her

head on Kristin's shoulder. "They put me in therapy after it happened. My dad was supposed to take me twice a week, but he forgot half of the time. He refused to go himself. He even told me once, when I asked him about it, pointing at the six-pack he was putting away, that it was all the therapy he needed, because my mother had been seeing a therapist for years and what good had it done her?" She finally put her glass down, keeping her head on Kristin's shoulder. "I stopped going. Between everyone's distress, and me splitting my time between living with my dad and living with my aunt, I was hard to keep track of. My dad didn't care. Didn't seem to at least. Then he didn't have to pay for it, I guess. More money for booze."

Despite never talking about it much, Kristin had often wondered, mostly while staring at Sheryl sleeping it off, what such neglect would do to a twelve-year-old girl. Sheryl might have had her aunt, but she no longer had her mother and the attention she needed from her father. To her surprise, Sheryl had always seemed so utterly composed. If she hadn't told her about her harrowing family history, Kristin would never have guessed.

To her dismay, she then realized it was one of the reasons why Kristin had never gotten too much on Sheryl's case about her ever-increasing thirst for alcohol. Sometimes she even caught herself thinking that if anyone deserved a drink, it was Sheryl. Sheryl who always held it together. The respected professor. The LGBT rights activist. The woman who believed in so much with such fervor, it had surprised and charmed Kristin in equal measures when they'd just started dating.

"There are people you can see now," Kristin said. "You don't have to go through this alone. You are not alone anymore." Kristin held her tighter, as if the closer she pressed Sheryl against her, the more she could bring this point across.

"I have you." Sheryl's tone, though injured, was

resolute.

Kristin couldn't help but wonder if she could ever be enough.

CHAPTER TWENTY-FOUR

Five days had gone by, and Sheryl hadn't done anything with the piece of paper. She'd stashed it away in a drawer in her desk, but out of sight was not out of mind.

She taught her classes, pretended to do research but nothing really got through, had meetings with her colleagues and office hours with her students. She sat around in The Pink Bean, watching people, and every time the door opened, with a flutter in her chest, she wondered if her father would walk in again. With all her might, she wanted life to continue the way it had before, but she couldn't shake the sight of him, and the memories it had ignited.

So, she drank. In a cruel reversal of everything she had believed in in her twenties. The only wish she'd had as a child—apart from being able to go back in time and being enough for her mother to not want to leave this world—had finally come true, now that her father had finally gotten sober. The irony didn't escape Sheryl, but what was she meant to do? Go to AA meetings with him?

Every night, after Kristin went to bed, Sheryl stayed up and easily polished off a bottle of wine, on top of the one she and Kristin had already shared over dinner. After the wine was finished, she turned to the bottle of vodka she kept in her desk—in a different drawer than her father's phone number.

Only after a few units of that, the liquor burning hard in her throat, its heat spreading through her, could she cope with the darkness of her bedroom. With the warmth of another person next to her. A woman who loved her. *Her.*

How was it even possible? It all felt like such a sham. In between knocking back shots, Sheryl asked herself the same questions over and over again: how had she managed to fool herself and everyone around her for so long? How had she found a woman who loved her? How could she respect a woman who could find it in her heart to do so when Sheryl had been utterly convinced, because the facts were so clear, since the age of twelve, that clearly she wasn't meant to be loved.

Most of all, though, she wondered how on earth she had managed to keep it together for so long. The will to survive, perhaps? Human nature? The surprising resilience of the mind and its ability to stash away in a dark corner what it doesn't want to remember?

Sheryl remembered now. She remembered her mother's arms around her, her voice always so sweet and low, when she said, "I should stop kissing you on this cheek. It will start showing on your skin." The love and warmth she had taken for granted, even when it became harder for her mother to muster an easy smile, and to get up to go to work in the morning.

Sheryl had been too young to understand any of it and perhaps too absorbed in her selfish early-teenage world, thus she'd had no way of bracing herself, of preparing herself for the worst.

Who did her father think he was, showing up like that? To him, it might have looked like an attempt to make amends; to Sheryl, it was the opposite. She *had* already made amends with her past. She had done the best she could with the hand that life had dealt her. She had found ways to forget, mechanisms to cope. Moreover, she had love. Stability. A beautiful partner. She had much more than she'd ever dreamed she'd have. And then this man walked into The Pink Bean... destroying it all.

She took another sip, while thinking of Kristin asleep in the other room. How could she explain to her how an old, deep wound, that had taken years to heal, had been brusquely torn open? And did she even have to? She slammed the glass down, noticing how sorry she was feeling for herself and hating the notion of it. This was not how Sheryl had picked herself up. When she was a child, wallowing in self-pity didn't even occur to her. So what the hell was she doing now? And why? Because nothing had changed. If it weren't for that persistent little voice in her head—her father's gruff baritone asking, "Please think about it."

———

"Professor Johnson," Martha said. "May I take a moment of your time?" She smiled disarmingly.

The last student hadn't closed the door, giving Martha ample opportunity to walk right in.

"Hey." An arrow of pain, which seemed to come from somewhere deep inside of her, burrowed its way up to Sheryl's temples. The headaches never stopped. "Sure." Sheryl gestured at a chair.

Martha closed the door. "You've been looking a bit pale of late," Martha said. "You know I have dibs on the fairer complexion." Her lips drew into a wide smile.

When Sheryl didn't reply, Martha's smile faded. "I'm officially worried now," she said. "Is it your health?"

"Not *my* health," Sheryl scoffed, then waved her hand. "Anyway, nothing for you to worry about. It will all blow over soon enough." That was the first time Sheryl allowed herself to wonder whether she was just waiting for her father to die, so she didn't have to make a decision anymore.

"Come on, Sheryl." Martha shifted nervously in her seat. It reminded Sheryl of that time she'd come into her office, much in the same way as today, and told her that she, too, was a lesbian. "I've never seen you like this. People are starting to talk."

"Who is *people*? Your ex-husband, the vice-chancellor, by any chance?"

"Colleagues who are just as worried about you as I am."

"How nice of them to worry." Sheryl ached to open her bottom drawer—the one where she hid another bottle of vodka. At first, she'd bought a bottle of Belvedere, because she wasn't going to get off her head on cheap, trashy booze, but the bottle was too long and didn't even fit into the cabinet under her desk. She'd soon switched to Absolut, a more modest brand of which the bottle fit neatly behind a stack of papers in her drawer.

"Hey, it's me you're talking to," Martha said. "Though I'm not entirely sure who *I* am talking to."

"I'm sorry," Sheryl said. "I've been going through some personal stuff."

"No kidding." Martha inclined her head. "And isn't that what friends are for?"

Sheryl considered this, and the friendships she'd had over the years. She had only ever briefly mentioned her family situation to Caitlin. Kristin knew more, but Sheryl refused to go into details. Was she really going to start now?

"Is it Kristin? Did something happen?"

Sheryl shook her head, though she'd done her best to push Kristin away. Kristin who had never once asked her an inappropriate question about her past. Who had never displayed anything but the utmost patience.

"It's something very personal." Sheryl tried to remember how she had ever found the words to tell Kristin, and how exactly she had said them. It seemed impossible to reproduce them now. God, she was thirsty. Her headache intensified, as did the foul taste in her mouth.

"Something to do with my family. It's complicated." She gazed at her hands. "Well, it's not really. It's my father. He's dying."

"I'm so sorry," Martha said. "No wonder you're upset."

Sheryl let her chin fall onto her chest. "It *is* actually more complicated than that." She looked up again. "How about we go for a drink and I tell you all about it?"

CHAPTER TWENTY-FIVE

"Look at them," Kristin said to Josephine, pointing at Micky and Robin who sat huddled together in a corner. "Doesn't young love look utterly silly at times?"

"I think it's sweet." Josephine gave her a smile. "And it's all down to this place."

"We should put it on the door," Kristin went along with the joke. She had to get her laughs wherever she could. The atmosphere in their home had turned glacial. "Hot beverages and matchmaking opportunities abound."

Josephine chuckled. "Their coffees are ready, but I almost don't want to disturb them."

"I'll take them." Kristin put the two cups on a tray and carried them over.

"One very wet cappuccino and one very dry," she said, sitting down at the table with them without waiting for an invitation.

"You'll never stop giving me hell about that, will you?" Robin said.

"No one ever will, babe," Micky said. Her eyes sparkled with the wild energy of falling in love. Finding Robin had taken ten years off of her, making Kristin feel very old in comparison.

Did Sheryl really think Kristin could fall asleep when she went to bed as Sheryl retreated into her office? Did she really believe that Kristin didn't know she hid a bottle of vodka in her drawer? Or was she waiting to be called out on it?

"Penny for your thoughts, boss," Micky said. They

worked together almost every day, surely she must have noticed something.

Kristin sighed. She was dying to talk about it, to have someone listen to her when she said something—Sheryl certainly didn't. But it wasn't for her to disclose. As far as Kristin knew, nobody but her and Caitlin knew about Sheryl's family history. Sheryl would be livid if Kristin told anyone—and rightly so.

"I haven't been sleeping too well," she said. She cast another glance at Micky and Robin, at the way they sat together, their bodies angled toward each other. It felt as though her and Sheryl's bodies were always pointing away from one another these days.

"Go upstairs and have a nap," Micky said. "I'll kick this one out—" She patted Robin on the knee. "—and get back to work. Josephine and I can handle things."

"Hey." Robin pretended to be offended. "I have to go, anyway. Diversity waits for no one."

"Not a bad idea," Kristin said, despite not being much of a day napper.

After saying her good-byes, she headed upstairs and walked around the apartment, where she went straight to Sheryl's office, as though following a hunch. The door was closed but not locked. They never locked the doors in the house. They didn't have reason to. An idea bloomed in the back of her mind—had probably been doing so for a while.

If Sheryl was going to be too stubborn, too depressed, or unraveling too much to do it, Kristin would do it for her. Sheryl wasn't going to give her answers anyway. She was bottling it all up, drinking her pain away.

Kristin had been in Sheryl's office when she'd seen her stash the piece of paper away in a drawer. She knew where to find Sheryl's father's phone number.

———

Kristin rang the bell. A thrill ran up her spine. Sheryl's father, Trevor, lived in Strathfield's Koreatown, an area she knew well. A second later, as if he'd been waiting on the other side, the door swung open.

"Kristin?" the man said.

"Yes." Kristin extended her hand. "Nice to meet you, Trevor."

"Come in." He opened the door and Kristin followed him into the apartment. The hallway was painted in an off-putting kind of brown and the small lounge, made up of what looked like secondhand furniture, didn't instill a cozy warmth in her either.

"Can I offer you some water? I'm afraid I don't have any coffee, turns out it's pretty bad for the liver as well." Trevor gave a rueful smile.

They sat down in a pair of knackered armchairs. Kristin tried to hide her nerves by sitting as still as possible. She only reached for the water glass after staring at her hands for a few seconds in silence and making sure they weren't trembling. The sense that she shouldn't be here made her jumpy. It felt like she was cheating on Sheryl by sitting across from this man, who looked nothing like Kristin had ever imagined him. Though, she suspected, time and substance abuse must have done a number on him.

Trevor Johnson's skin was almost translucent, with purplish half moons underneath his eyes. Whatever he had left of his hair was combed backward but didn't hide the liver spots dotting his skull. What Kristin noticed most were his hands, bony and thin-fingered, which kept fidgeting with nothing.

"How's Sheryl?" he asked right off the bat.

"Not well." Kristin examined his face, looking for similarities between it and her partner's. Perhaps the eyes a little bit, though Trevor's were watery and heavy-lidded and Kristin could barely see the blue shine through. "Not since you showed up." She tried to keep any blame out of her voice. That wasn't why she had come.

The only reason she had ventured all this way, risking

Sheryl's wrath, was because she was desperate to understand. To meet someone in Sheryl's family, the woman she had spent the better part of her life with. The woman she had asked to elope with her to New Zealand to marry a few years ago, but who had refused on principle as long as the Australian government *kept its head up its ass* on the matter. A no that hadn't hurt Kristin in the slightest because she understood the reason behind it.

"It wasn't an easy decision to look Sheryl up." Trevor's head shook a little. "In the end, I felt I had no choice. If only to tell her that none of what happened was her fault. She was only a child when Maureen died, and I was so off my head all the time, I might as well have died along with her." He stroked the stubble on his chin. "Do you think it was too selfish of me to contact her like that?"

Kristin was taken aback by that question. Not only because she hadn't expected it, but also because Trevor seemed to possess the same inquisitive nature Sheryl had.

"Not really," she replied. "But it shocked Sheryl and ripped open all those old wounds. Made her think of the childhood she could have had, perhaps. All the missed opportunities." Kristin cleared her throat. She glanced at Trevor who looked at her intently, lips slightly pursed. "I've known Sheryl for a very long time, and she's never done self-pity. Until you turned up. It has shaken her to the core, and for someone who is impossible to shut up at times, she's being awfully quiet about it all."

His lips drew into a smile. "That sounds like Sheryl all right. The not being able to shut up part. She was always like that. Always debating at the dinner table, ever since she was a little girl." He shook his head. "All I wanted was some reassurance that she did okay in life. That I hadn't messed her up too badly. I had one of the guys I share this apartment with, a younger fella, look her up on the internet, and I was very impressed when he told me she's a professor. I could immediately see it, you know? Despite having been absent from her life for so long, if I had any working brain cells left"—a guileless chuckle—"that's what I would have guessed. Smart as a whip, that girl." His voice broke a little.

"She's a wonderful woman." Kristin hadn't expected to be moved so much by the sight of this man's emotions. She found it hard to be angry at him. Perhaps because most of what happened between him and Sheryl did so before they met.

"I let her down in every way. I couldn't cope. I was a weak, weak man instead of the father Sheryl needed so much at that time. I don't deserve even a minute of her time, I know that. But I don't have much time left and… she's all I think about. Time is rapidly running out for me. Ironically, when you've been a drunk most of your life and then become sober, time is all you seem to have. And I spend every second of it thinking about my daughter. Regretting the poor choices I made when she needed me most." He drummed his fingers on the armrest. "Does Sheryl know you're here?"

Kristin shook her head. "No, but I will tell her. We're not the sort to keep secrets from each other."

"You seem like a lovely woman. I'm glad Sheryl found someone like you. Nothing can ever make me feel better about how I behaved, but knowing that she's with someone as kind and understanding as yourself gives me a little bit of relief from my regrets."

Kristin was baffled by the eloquence of the man. Shouldn't forty years of alcohol abuse have left him more of a wreck? Hands shaking and eyes leaking tears inadvertently. The occasional coherent sentence making it through a barrage of nonsense. He really was Sheryl's father all right.

"Will you… will you please tell her how sorry I am for everything? And that I don't expect anything from her. I've already gotten more than I dreamed I would by having this chat with you." Trevor's face contorted into a grimace. He shifted in his seat and reached for his glass of water. "I'm already more at peace."

"I'll do my best." Kristin guessed he must be in pain, the way he angled his body to one side and his eyes narrowed. "I'd better go now." She rose, and when Trevor started pushing himself out of his chair, she lifted her hand. "Don't get up, I'll see myself out." She held out her hand, and he put his shakily in hers. Kristin cast him one last glance, and it seemed that, during their ten-minute conversation, he had aged twenty years.

CHAPTER TWENTY-SIX

"I told Martha about my father," Sheryl mumbled.

Kristin's eyes went wide. Sheryl had stumbled in, nearly knocking over the porcelain statue—a Park family heirloom —on the cabinet where she kept her keys. Kristin had immediately known it would not be a good night to tell Sheryl that she'd met her father. Even if she did, Sheryl probably wouldn't remember in the morning.

"You did?" She tried to keep her voice level, even tried to inject some encouragement into her tone, even though it was hard. Seeing Sheryl like that made her feel so completely powerless.

"We went for a drink." Sheryl scrunched her lips together. "I know I've had a few too many." She leaned lopsidedly against the cabinet. "You can blame Martha for that. And Trevor. You can blame him as well."

Kristin supposed she should at least be glad Sheryl had opened up to someone, though she would have preferred it to be her. The conversation Sheryl had had with Martha had probably been more informative than the emotional one they needed to have between them. She tried to look on the bright side. Sheryl must be in a talkative mood.

"I'm not blaming anyone." Kristin walked over to Sheryl, the way she had done so many times lately, and took her by the hand, leading her to the sofa. "Let's sit for a bit."

"I'm so, so tired." Sheryl leaned half her body weight onto Kristin.

"I'll make some coffee." Kristin deposited Sheryl in her preferred spot and went into the kitchen. She was of half a mind to call Martha and ask her how she could have left Sheryl, who was her friend, in such a state. She appeared much more out of it than usual. Sheryl definitely drank in public, but she was smart enough—Kristin heard Trevor's words echo in her head: *smart as a whip, that girl*—to never let herself go too much until she got home. Until after Kristin had gone to bed even. As though drinking to such excess was a purely personal affair.

When Kristin brought the coffee over—decaf for herself—Sheryl sat slumped, her chin tucked into her chest, hands hanging loosely by her side, eyes closed. She probably was too far gone to have any kind of conversation with. Everything would have to be postponed to tomorrow again, the way it had been for almost a week now.

Kristin doubted Sheryl would make it into work tomorrow. Maybe they could finally talk then.

Kristin sipped from the scalding hot coffee while she listened to Sheryl's breathing. She put down her cup, took off Sheryl's shoes, negotiated her out of her jacket, and pushed her down until she looked like she was in a somewhat comfortable position. Kristin propped a cushion beneath her neck and draped the blanket she'd been watching television under, while waiting for Sheryl to come home, over her.

She bent down, kissed her on the cheek, braving the toxic smell of alcohol on her breath, and said, "I love you."

Sheryl just kept on snoring.

Kristin looked at Sheryl for a few minutes before finding her phone and texting Martha: *What state was Sheryl in when she left?*

She erased the message before she could press send. None of this was Martha's fault.

———

Sheryl woke with the familiar torrent of shame and disgust racing through her. Her body felt like she'd taken a severe beating the night before. She looked around, trying to get her bearings. A cup of steaming coffee stood right in her line of sight. She glanced upward a bit more and looked into Kristin's face.

"I called your office," Kristin said. "Told them you were too ill to even pick up the phone yourself and let them know you wouldn't be in today."

"What time is it?" Sheryl swung her legs out too quickly and a dizzy spell overtook her.

"Nine." Kristin didn't look too pleased.

Sheryl tried to remember if she had said anything when she'd come home last night that would have put Kristin in this mood. Then she concluded that it probably wasn't so much about last night, but all the previous nights combined.

"Whether you want to or not, today you and I are going to talk." Kristin used the tone of voice she reserved for very special, solemn occasions. The one that didn't tolerate any backtalk.

Sheryl could only nod. She needed a shower and a triple dose of Ibuprofen. She made do with the coffee for now.

"This has to stop, Sheryl. I barely recognize you." The earlier solemn note in Kristin's voice had made way for raw concern.

"I know." Sheryl's voice sounded as though she had smoked an entire sleeve of cigarettes the night before. "I'm sorry."

"I went to see your father yesterday," Kristin said, her voice loud and clear.

Sheryl had heard what she'd said perfectly, but had trouble absorbing the statement. "You did what?"

"I called him and went to his house." She studied her nails, then looked back up at Sheryl.

"Behind my back?" Sheryl's pounding headache made way for panic. Kristin must have gone through her desk drawers to find the number. She must have found the bottle of vodka. Why hadn't she stashed it somewhere more original? Behind a couple of books on the shelf.

"You're falling apart, babe." Nothing but worry in Kristin's voice. "I felt I—I needed to do something, even if that included going behind your back."

"You went through my stuff." Sheryl tried to push herself out of the sofa, but her legs didn't cooperate. Kristin was clever, cornering her upon waking.

"For which I apologize, but I'd seen you put away the piece of paper with his number on it. I knew where to look."

Perhaps Kristin hadn't found the bottle. Sheryl didn't know why establishing this fact was so important to her, but it was. Having Kristin happen upon a hidden bottle like that would be too humiliating, too much hard evidence of what was going on—evidence of Sheryl's failure and how she was dealing with her past.

"You should have talked to me first." Sheryl made circular motions with her fingers around her temples.

"I know, but you made that impossible. You shut down completely after he came here." Kristin rose from her seat and sat next to her. "I didn't do it to hurt you, on the contrary. But I couldn't sit on the sidelines any longer, watching you destroy yourself."

A phone started ringing close by, its shrill sound making Sheryl jump. They both looked around.

"It's yours," Kristin said. She reached over to the other end of the sofa and fished it out of Sheryl's jacket pocket.

"I don't want to talk to anyone." Sheryl waved it off.

"It's Martha." Kristin handed her the phone.

"I'll talk to her later." Sheryl dismissed the call. She tried to remember what she had told Martha last night. Had she broken down in The Flying Pig? And how on earth had she gotten home?

"I have a bone to pick with her," Kristin said. "The state you were in last night." There was an edge to Kristin's tone.

They both took a breath, Sheryl's long and deep and

shuddering.

"It was hard. Seeing him. Him talking to me," she said. "At first, it felt like just a man sitting across from me, but he isn't just some old codger. He's my father. A man who was supposed to love me and make me feel safe, but failed me so spectacularly. And I don't know what to do with that."

Kristin shuffled a little closer. Sheryl wished she wouldn't. She needed space. To breathe and to think. To finally deal with the sudden enormity of all the things she had never dealt with.

"I know." Kristin slung an arm around her shoulders. "I know it's hard, but not talking to me and… and hiding in your office all night long isn't going to make things better."

"I don't know whether I love or hate him," Sheryl blurted out.

"Probably a bit of both." Kristin squeezed her shoulder tighter. "But what have you truly got to lose by getting in touch with him?" Kristin asked. "That you haven't lost already?"

———

"I just don't think he deserves it," Sheryl said. She spoke in a tone that Kristin had seldom heard, a hangover mixed with extreme emotions underlying her words. Just like she'd seen Trevor age in front of her eyes during the timespan of a short conversation, Sheryl seemed to have grown smaller, her hair a little grayer, her wrinkles deeper. "Why should he deserve to die with my forgiveness?"

"He doesn't, but it's not really about that." Kristin tried to feel her way through this conversation. She didn't so much try to say the right things, but avoid the wrong ones. Sheryl was slowly opening up. All her defenses were down. Perhaps it was cruel to pounce on her as soon as she'd opened her eyes, but Kristin couldn't watch her in agony one day longer. Sheryl wasn't going to help herself, so it was up to Kristin to step in. Knowing that she was doing the right thing, didn't make it easier, though. "This is about you."

Kristin paused. She'd been up most of the night while Sheryl slept it off, thinking about how to deliver the next phrase. The one it all came down to. The one that could, quite possibly, send Sheryl into a frenzied anger that she wouldn't snap out of any time soon. "About what this has been doing to you. The drinking, babe."

Sheryl didn't say anything. She pushed the heels of her hands against her eyes. When she removed them, she turned her face away from Kristin. "That's why, apart from it being such a shock, it was so hard to see him. I saw all my own faults reflected back at me." A sniffle escaped her.

Kristin moved her hand to Sheryl's neck and gently massaged her. The feel of her fingers on Sheryl's skin reminded her of how little they had touched each other of late.

"In a way, I've become him. The very worst part of him." Sheryl turned to face Kristin. Her eyes were red-rimmed and full of tears. "The exact thing I never wanted to be."

"You haven't," Kristin said. "You're an entirely different person."

Sheryl shook her head. "Am I?" Her voice shot up. "I used to sit in a chair watching him the way you sat watching me this morning. Waiting for him to wake up, after I'd gone through his pockets to find some money so I could buy myself some breakfast. More often than not, there wasn't any left and he sent me to the ATM when he woke up."

"You are not like your father, babe," Kristin insisted. "He was an alcoholic for thirty-five years. I would never let you become that."

"Because I have you and he had no one." Sheryl shrugged violently. "Well, he had me, but I was powerless."

"The situation is so very different." Kristin tried to look Sheryl in the eye, but it was impossible to hold her gaze, which kept skittering away.

"Maybe you're right," Sheryl said. "Maybe I have no

choice but to go and see him." She let out a long breath. "I'd best not wait too long if I want to have my say before he kicks the bucket."

CHAPTER TWENTY-SEVEN

Sheryl had let Kristin set up the meeting, and she was letting her drive to her father's place as well. It had happened fast, not only because Trevor had claimed he didn't have long, but also because, if given too much time, Sheryl might have backed out. She didn't want more hours to ruminate on it. To balance the pros and cons. To analyze the data the way she did after conducting a research survey. Her feelings were not data and her sad past had been analyzed to death already.

When they pulled up to the curb and Kristin parked the car, the doubts she'd been having since she'd given Kristin permission to call her father intensified. But she knew it was just nerves. Because now she was meeting her father on her own terms. There was no surprise effect to subdue the buried emotions that were bound to surface.

It seemed like ages since she'd woken up on the sofa and Kristin had told her about calling him, even though it had only been that same morning. But Sheryl knew that having a night in between, and her nights these days were either sleepless or severely drunk, would have her back out. She'd spent the day fighting the urge to drink and crying on Kristin's shoulder. And now there she sat, ready to get out of the car and ring his doorbell, and she was already so spent.

Trevor looked different than when he'd shown up at The Pink Bean. Older. His skin a harsh yellow. Sheryl couldn't help but wonder if he'd fallen off the wagon. She breathed in deeply—the smell of a house where too much alcohol

191

was consumed would never leave her—but didn't detect the faintest whiff of that particular acrid odor she used to come home to from school.

Her father looked like the very definition of a man whose days were numbered. He walked through the house slowly, his movements measured and minute, and Kristin soon took on the task of fetching water from the kitchen and pouring them each a glass, leaving Sheryl alone with her father in the lounge for a few uncomfortable minutes.

She had never guessed that, when the time came for this moment, she would need Kristin by her side so desperately.

"Do you live here alone?" Sheryl asked, looking around the room.

Her father shook his head. "I have two flatmates. I asked them to give us some privacy," he whispered.

Sheryl had to strain to hear. Of course Trevor had aged, lost the paunch she'd always remembered him carrying around the waist, and looked like a ghost of the man he used to be, but what had changed most dramatically was his voice. If he had ever bothered to call her, Sheryl wouldn't have recognized him by hearing it alone.

Kristin emerged from the kitchen, and Sheryl had rarely been gladder to see her. Her father could quite possibly be the only person in this world she didn't know how to talk to.

"I'm glad you came," Trevor said after they'd all sat down.

"You don't look too well," Kristin said. "Should we take you to a doctor later?" There was genuine worry in her voice.

Trevor shook his head. "There's nothing left that a doctor could do for me."

"When you said you didn't have long." Sheryl managed to keep all emotion from her voice. "What time frame are we talking about? Weeks? Months?"

"Weeks," Trevor whispered. "If not days, what with the way I'm feeling today."

Sheryl refrained from rolling her eyes. No matter what else he had lost, Trevor was still in full possession of his dramatic streak. Though, truth be told, he did look like death was about to knock on his door.

"We won't keep you long," Sheryl said. It came out much crueler than she had intended.

"Is there anything we can do?" Kristin asked. Sheryl guessed she was saying it partly to make up for Sheryl's snide remark and partly because she just couldn't help being a Good Samaritan.

"That's very kind of you." Trevor blinked slowly. "Being here is more than enough."

The elemental rage Sheryl felt at seeing him, at having to talk to him, warred with the pity she couldn't help but feel for him—and for herself. It also made her realize that, over the years, she'd had ample opportunity to get in touch. To check in and see if her father had changed. Perhaps she had always known that if the time was right for him, he would find her.

"I'm sorry for not being there," he started to say. "I'm sorry for not being able to control my—"

Sheryl held up her hand. This might very well be the last time she saw her father. Hearing him apologize wasn't going to make a fundamental difference in her life. He had looked her up. She knew he was sorry. Of course he was. Sheryl wasn't the kind of person who needed it spelled out for her. Most of all, she wanted to get out of that darkened room where dust motes hung in the thin shaft of light that was allowed in. This house with her father's presence in it was oppressing, was sucking any joy right out of her—and she already had so little left.

"I don't want your apologies." That harsh tone again. She corrected herself. "I just want to know why. Why Mom did it and why... you didn't step up for me."

Trevor nodded thoughtfully. He looked like he was weighing his words—perhaps he had only a limited amount left, like days in his life.

"I—" Trevor started, but Sheryl wouldn't let him. The sound of his powerless voice suddenly irked her, as though it represented his entire existence in her life. He'd been powerless to be her father after her mother's death and now it was all there—the memories, the sadness, the questions Sheryl couldn't help but ask herself—in his useless, breathless voice.

"The note she left me was so brief," Sheryl said. "It didn't give any explanation." Sheryl hadn't allowed herself to think of her mother's good-bye note for a long time. She kept it in a plastic folder in a drawer at work. Having it at home always seemed too much somehow. "It just said that hopefully one day, when I was older, I would understand."

It wasn't understanding Sheryl lacked. She had scoured the university library for any book she could find on clinical depression, and had them order any new one even remotely related to the subject. When it came to cold hard facts, she knew why her mother had taken her own life. What she couldn't wrap her head around was why, if things had gotten so bad that a mother was willing to leave her daughter behind, to have her fend for herself in a world she herself was so desperate and determined to leave, her father hadn't done anything about it. Had her admitted. Dragged her to counseling. Cut the noose from around her fucking neck before she choked to death.

Trevor shook his head. Perhaps he'd already lost the power of speech entirely. Then he cleared his throat again. "I can never give you a satisfactory answer to that question, Sheryl. Your mother did what she did because she felt it was the only way for her. As for me… I spent the rest of my life trying to drown my grief. There are no excuses for that."

"For the longest time, I didn't know which one of the two of you I should hate the most." Sheryl's voice boomed through the room. She wasn't speaking that loudly, but the contrast with her father's throaty whisper was too big. "But Mom was dead and I did everything in my power to grasp the immense blackness she faced every day. And despite the note she left me, I will never fully understand what that must have been like, but at least I didn't have to see her suffer and wither away the way I did with you. I didn't have to witness how she wrecked herself a little more every single day. You were still alive, but you might as well not have been."

"I couldn't forgive her for what she had done. I just couldn't." Trevor's tone had grown a bit more powerful. "The only way for me to deal with it was by escaping myself."

Sheryl expressed a loud sigh. "And where did that leave me?"

"No place good." A tremor in his voice, like he was about to cry. "Every day was double agony for me. I despised your mother, the woman I loved, for being such a coward, and I despised myself for being so powerless.

"Powerless to help her and powerless to help you and myself in the aftermath. Booze became my best friend, and I just let myself slide down that slippery slope all the way. I have been an appalling father and husband in every respect. A despicable man with no pride or dignity left."

His speech left him gasping for air.

"Oh yes, you're such a martyr," Sheryl said. "At least you were out of it most of the time. I was only a child. A twelve-year-old with no options whatsoever."

"I know. And there's nothing I can say or do that will ever change that."

Sheryl couldn't look at him anymore. If he died tomorrow, it would be a relief. Then she could go back to the life she had built for herself, despite all the odds stacked against her. She could shake off these bouts of deplorable self-pity that came over her. Maybe she could even stop drinking, now that she had an up-close reminder of what it could do to a person. She didn't want to turn into a groveling, regretful shell of a human being.

Sheryl didn't need anymore regrets. She didn't need anymore conversations with this man who was, by blood, her father, but was by no other means connected to her. If anything, she could learn from his mistake. Though, even as she was still sitting there, rapidly being consumed by the anger she had managed to keep at bay, she already knew that her inclination toward a few drinks was not something even the sight of her pathetic father could snap her out of, because all she wanted was a large glass of wine or a shot of vodka burning down her throat, or both.

Sheryl looked at Kristin. She hadn't noticed until now, but her eyes were wet with tears. Did she somehow owe it to the woman she loved to stay? To give Trevor assurances about her life and her levels of happiness? What could she even say? *We're happy, though things could be better. I'm turning into the same vile alcoholic that you were, now that you've gotten sober. How's that for irony?*

"I need to get out of here." Sheryl rose. "Just… for a walk or something."

Kristin stood up as well. Trevor stayed seated. If Sheryl were to etch any visual in her brain forever after coming to this house, it would be the pained expression on his face. Sunken blue eyes, dark purple bags underneath them. Hollow cheeks and lips so pale no color could describe them. All of it combining in a look of a guilt so extreme, Sheryl wondered if it wasn't that eating him alive, instead of his liver failing. She guessed a bit of both.

"Just give me a minute. I'll be back." She waved off Kristin, feeling sorry for leaving her alone with her father, but it wouldn't be the first time after all.

———

As she walked around the streets of Strathfield where she'd never been, Sheryl pondered forgiveness. Or, at least, trying to mimic it for a few minutes for the sake of her dying father. She had three options: not going back into his house and never speaking to him again; going back, saying something vague about having created a life well beyond any expectations her youth might have prescribed; and going back, looking him in the watery, fading eyes again, and trying to find something in her, a flicker of goodness, of love for a father she barely knew, and consider giving him what he really wanted: a piece of herself.

She sucked her lungs full of air, as though fresh oxygen had all the answers. She kept her face to the ground, to her feet falling onto the sidewalk, and thought about her mother. In the beginning, she'd looked at pictures of her, of the two of them, every day. She wondered what she would look like now, if she had lived. Would she have looked like Sheryl when she was fifty? Did it still matter? Sheryl was forty-seven; she'd lived thirty-five years without a mother. About the same without a father. She'd only ever had herself. This decision too, came down to herself, and to the person she had become.

She asked herself how she would want to have acted after it was too late. When she stood over his casket at his funeral—perhaps, if Trevor was telling the truth, only days away. If she went at all. She could choose to stay at home and drink instead, but even Sheryl's jaded sense of irony couldn't stretch that far. Would she break down? Regret not having spoken to him again? Or would her soul be wrapped in steel forever?

She passed by a bottle shop and, without even thinking about it, went inside. She looked around and decided on a can of Victoria Bitter, a large one. She took it outside and scanned her surroundings for a place to sit and drink. To think. When she couldn't immediately find anywhere more suitable, she sank down to the curb in front of the bottle shop and, before opening the can, wondered if she was being the spitting image her father. Did he sit like this on sidewalks getting wasted? Or was that too much of a cliché image of the alcoholic? Either way, as she sat there, pulled the lid off the can, and brought it to her lips, she could get a sense of his pain. Yes, he had been weak, and he had abandoned her in the worst way, making Sheryl believe that neither one of her parents loved her enough; all of that had happened and was unequivocally true. But Trevor hadn't deserted her for no reason, and some shoulders weren't built to carry that amount of pain and grief. He had made one wrong decision after another to numb his pain, and perhaps it had worked and drowned out a small percentage of it. But, Sheryl knew from experience, once he'd slept it off, the pain would have come back hard and fast and unrelenting, clobbering him half to death again. Every single day of his life. And who was she to judge?

She took one last sip of the can, crumpled it up still half full, and tossed it in the bin. Perhaps the truth had lain in a can of beer all along, because what Sheryl knew as she made her way back to her father's house, was that to beat her own demons, she would need to find a way to forgive the man who had pushed her in this direction most. It wouldn't happen today. Maybe not even before he died. But no matter how long it took, it was the only way.

CHAPTER TWENTY-EIGHT

"We can cancel the dinner," Kristin said. "Tell everyone you have a family emergency."

"And do what?" Sheryl half shouted from the living room. "Eat all the food you bought ourselves?"

And drink the wine, Kristin thought. She glanced over at the wine fridge, which still held a couple of vintage bottles from her time with Sterling Wines, and was always fully stocked. She walked into the living room and sat down next to Sheryl.

"We can make it an alcohol-free dinner," she said.

Sheryl shook her head. "This is my problem, not anyone else's."

"No, it's not." Kristin looked into Sheryl's blue eyes. "Your friends will support you. You don't have to do this alone."

"Maybe not on the surface, but really, what can my friends do for me? How can they deal with stuff that is so inherently mine?"

"By showing their support and abstaining from drinking around you. At least in the beginning."

"Abstinence is not my goal." Sheryl straightened her shoulders. "I think moderation is more realistic."

Kristin quirked up her eyebrows. "You do?" After they'd left Trevor's house, Sheryl had made a few bold claims, like vowing to give up alcohol and sort out the mess in her head that drove her to the bottle and even try to find it somewhere in her heart to forgive her father, but Kristin had seen through all of that easily. Sheryl was processing the conversation with her father, the memories it had brought up, and dreaming up a better version of herself to be able to deal with it all better.

Though certainly the most realistic option, Kristin wasn't quite sure moderation was the best solution in the long run, because of the bigger risk of a relapse.

Sheryl nodded earnestly. "I've been racking my brain trying to pinpoint when drinking became more to me than just a way to unwind, a way to bond with my friends, but I can't for the life of me remember. I remember the time when I was always the one with half a glass of wine in front of me and barely touching it, and I remember when, after pouring myself that first glass, I was already looking forward to the second, but no stage in between."

Kristin tried to remember as well but had to admit that she had probably been too busy at work to notice. While she knew it was foolish to blame herself, even partly, for Sheryl's drinking, she couldn't help but feel a tiny flicker of guilt every time they addressed the issue.

"Like most things in life, it happened gradually. Without us even noticing." Though Kristin could still vividly remember the shocking discovery of the supermarket receipt for that ghastly bottle of red wine Sheryl had bought for herself, to drink behind Kristin's back while she was at work. She *had* noticed then, but hadn't spoken up. Because life had gotten in the way, as usual, and, back then, it was somehow easier to believe that her partner of so many years was finding some comfort in a cheap bottle of wine when Kristin's arms weren't available.

"I'm pretty certain the whole process isn't reversible," Sheryl said with a sigh. "But I can try." She looked away for a minute, through the window. "It's been two days now. I look forward to a drink." As if admitting this out loud had triggered an immediate physical reaction, her leg started jittering.

Kristin had the time now, and she was the person who

knew Sheryl best, but she had no idea how to deal with this. All she knew was what she wanted to avoid at all cost: Sheryl locking herself into her office with a bottle of vodka and not coming out until she was shit-faced. To have to see her like that again would break her heart all over again. There was a big difference between seeing the woman you love tipsy at a party, breaking out in serious speeches about women's rights and the direction modern-day feminism is taking, and witnessing how all zest for life had drained from her eyes, from her entire body, and been replaced by the numbing, crushing effects of alcohol.

"Do you think that you could perhaps benefit from some outside help?" Kristin didn't have the heart to look at Sheryl's face after suggesting this.

"You mean AA?" Sheryl's voice remained steady.

"Or therapy."

"Perhaps," Sheryl said. "Therapy, not AA." She leaned back in the sofa. "I'm not sure I want to stop drinking entirely. I like the buzz of a couple of drinks. The way a glass of wine tastes different on a Friday night when the weekend begins. I love pouring a nice bottle for our friends when we have a dinner party."

"I know you do." Kristin understood the joy of all these little pleasures perfectly. "But the very nature of alcohol makes you lose control over when to stop." They had tried Sheryl relying on subtle—or not so subtle—cues from Kristin before to curb her drinking enthusiasm. It hadn't worked.

"So you think I should stop? Go cold turkey?"

Kristin knew she couldn't win here, but this conversation had to continue. She had stopped it at crucial times too often before. "With professional help. Yes."

"You think it truly is an addiction and not just a temporary reaction to things from my past?"

"It has escalated with your father showing up, but you were not exactly in control of your habit for quite a few years before."

"And when you say habit, you mean addiction," Sheryl said matter-of-factly.

"I don't know, babe. That's the point I'm trying to make. How can we, just the two of us, ever truly figure this out?"

"I know I said I would quit." Sheryl's voice was starting to lose its confident note. "But saying it is so much easier than actually doing it."

"I know." Kristin nodded thoughtfully, hoping Sheryl would soon reach the inevitable conclusion. "I will support you. I'll get rid of all the alcohol in the house. I won't drink a drop until you're comfortable with me doing so, but I won't drink in our home. We'll do this together."

"I don't want you to make that kind of a sacrifice for me." A sudden harshness in Sheryl's tone. "I don't need you to."

"It's not a sacrifice at all." She shuffled a little closer to Sheryl. "Seeing you sober and happy and healthy will give me a million times more pleasure than a sip of the greatest wine."

"You say that now." Sheryl put a hand on Kristin's knee and squeezed softly.

"I mean it." Kristin leaned in, ready to kiss Sheryl on the cheek.

Sheryl pulled away and said, "I just don't see myself as an addict. I don't see myself counting days without booze and collecting a chip after reciting the serenity prayer. I don't even pray."

"Then we'll find you a therapist who specializes in..." Why was it still so hard to say those words out loud? "Substance abuse."

Sheryl heaved a big sigh. "One last drink?" Her eyes lit up. "Or one last blowout with our friends tomorrow at the dinner party?"

Kristin shook her head. "Why waste the two sober days

you've already had?"

"Because…" Sheryl leaned away farther from Kristin. "I want to."

"Let's just try." Kristin didn't let up; she couldn't afford to. "I'll let everyone know no wine will be served and they shouldn't bring any either."

"That's like sharing it with all of them. I'm not sure I'm ready for that."

"They're our friends. They know you."

"What's that supposed to mean? They know I'm a drunk?"

"They know you're prone to having one too many. It's just one dinner. They will support you."

"I'm not sure about this." Sheryl's entire posture deflated.

"I understand." Kristin shuffled closer still, trying to bridge the gap Sheryl had been putting between them. "But it will be so much easier for you to resist a drink if nobody else is having one. Why make it harder for yourself than it has to be?"

"Because, aside from asking my friends to spend a perfectly good Saturday night abstaining, I will, by doing so, also be admitting to my own weakness. That's hard."

"But isn't that what friends are for? To be there for you in hard times?"

Sheryl still had a reluctant furrow in her brow. "And Amber, the only person who would happily not drink, won't even be there."

Kristin pictured Amber meditating on a mountain with a staggering view wherever in India she was. They could do with someone like Amber right about now. Someone who only drank for show, and wasn't afraid to lay out all the reasons, over and over again, why alcohol was bad for you. But, even more so, someone who had all the tools necessary to help Sheryl find the peace of mind she'd so sorely been lacking for years.

"I know I haven't always made the best decisions for our life and our relationship, but I have learned from my mistakes." Kristin hadn't meant to sound so formal. "I'm asking you to trust me. I will arrange everything for tomorrow; we won't even have to talk about it if you don't want to."

"No." Sheryl's voice rang firm. "I don't want that kind of tension and I believe in the power of transparent communication. If we're doing this, then it's all going to be out in the open."

"Okay." Kristin nodded, finally pecked Sheryl on the cheek, while a little sliver of hope crept up her spine.

CHAPTER TWENTY-NINE

Even before any guests had arrived, Sheryl wanted nothing more than to open a bottle of wine. It had always been such an act of anticipation: letting a bottle of excellent wine breathe so it would be perfect and ready for when their friends arrived.

But there was no more wine to be found in their apartment. With cheeks turning a telltale pink, Sheryl had surrendered one half-empty and one full bottle of vodka she'd stashed away in her desk drawer, and had watched Kristin drain them into the sink.

Kristin had sent Sheryl to the farmer's market to pick up vegetables for tonight, and when Sheryl had returned, the smell of wine was unmistakable in the flat, leading Sheryl to believe that Kristin had poured away the not-so-good bottles in the sink as well. Sheryl had no idea what she had done with the expensive ones, and she hadn't asked.

Sheryl had inhaled deeply while depositing her shopping bag on the kitchen counter, but Kristin hadn't given her a chance to say anything. Instead she had pressed her lips hard against Sheryl's. When Sheryl had let her hands run down Kristin's sides, then underneath her top, Kristin had swatted them away, telling her not to distract the chef too much.

Since The Pink Bean had found its groove and Kristin's presence downstairs was less and less required, she had made the kitchen her domain. Because she was a woman who succeeded at most things she put her mind to, she had soon started turning out stunning dishes and dinner parties had become more frequent.

Kristin was the kind of independent home cook who didn't much tolerate company in the kitchen, and Sheryl usually spent time in her office or downstairs. But that day Kristin had involved her in the cooking, and only raised an eyebrow when Sheryl hadn't diced the carrots the way she had wanted her to do.

It had been an enjoyable day. It could have been an ordinary one, if it weren't for the nerves running through Sheryl at the prospect of entertaining without the support of alcohol. She had somehow forgotten to hold court like that, even though well into the first years of their relationship, Sheryl did it all the time. She had never needed alcohol. She had despised and stayed away from it and doing so hadn't had any adverse impact on her life.

Martha was the first to arrive, a bunch of tulips in her hand. She was soon followed by Micky and Robin, who offered her, upon opening the door, a bouquet of roses.

Sheryl refrained from making a snide comment—something along the lines of "do they come with a commiseration card, saying how sorry you are for my loss of alcohol?"—and dutifully put them in a vase.

Kristin had—of course—researched virgin cocktail recipes and while Kristin plated the hors d'oeuvres in the kitchen, Sheryl served their guests kumquat spritzers with pomegranate seeds in cocktail glasses. As she did, she couldn't help but wonder who was secretly wishing for a shot of something stronger on the side.

"When is Amber coming back?" Martha asked Micky.

"I'm not entirely sure," Micky said. "She keeps extending her stay."

"She must have a lot to think about." Robin sipped from her drink and, Sheryl could swear, pulled one of those disgusted faces that are entirely involuntary.

"She'd be much better off thinking less about almost everything," Micky said. "But it's who she is." She gave

Martha a look that bordered on pity—one, Sheryl knew, Martha would not take well.

"We can only wait patiently for the return of our great yogi." Sheryl stood around awkwardly with a carafe of what was basically funny-colored juice in her hands.

It was that exact moment that she needed a drink the most. Just a little something to take the edge off. To lubricate her tongue and steer the conversation the way she was used to doing, without qualms or hesitation. She cleared her throat, sensing that the subject of an alcohol-free dinner should be addressed properly, but just then Kristin walked into the lounge with a platter of miniature quiches, and all three guests cooed.

"You're not asking them to give up a limb or ignore a vital part of their personality," Kristin had assured her the day before, "just by requesting them not to drink. It really isn't such a big deal."

Perhaps it wasn't. In theory, Kristin was right. But why did everything feel so off? Why did Sheryl feel like she was depriving her friends of the required relaxation a Saturday night merited, as though it all depended on how strong the booze was? If anything, Sheryl thought, as she headed into the kitchen to put the carafe in the fridge—Kristin had suggested an ice bucket, but Sheryl had believed that to look too ridiculous—she should be happy she had friends who were willing to consider a night like this. Awful though it sounded, she knew for a fact that proposing an alcohol-free Saturday evening wouldn't go down well in most groups of friends in Australia. Everyone had their own excuse to drink, perhaps not as much as she did, and not with the same consequences, but all the same, Australians liked their booze. And, thank goodness for their blooming business, their coffee the morning after.

She remembered the oft-spoken words, like a chant the morning after, amongst her college friends, back in the LAUS days. "A coffee, a painkiller, and no whining allowed.

Hangovers are for wimps." Back then, they'd barely felt the negative effects, and Sheryl had missed her body's prime time for drinking excessively.

———————

At any other previous dinner party, Sheryl was always firmly planted in her seat, while Kristin did all the running around. Kristin had never minded because it was the natural flow of events that matched their respective personalities. She'd much rather hear Sheryl challenge Micky on visibility as an out lesbian, or cause Martha to shuffle nervously in her chair while she tried to come up with a reply that matched Sheryl's quick wit, than have her serve the fish course. Kristin was the cook; Sheryl the entertainer. Except tonight.

Rather clumsily, Sheryl insisted on carrying out the starters of seafood terrine, even though Kristin had spent a long time plating them and they required a steady hand to transport them from kitchen to dining table. Sheryl's hands looked anything but steady. She was twitchy, stroking her chin nonstop, even curling a strand of hair around her finger once in a while—a gesture Kristin had never witnessed before.

It was expected that Sheryl would be off her game, and conversation might not be as fluid as they were used to, but Kristin had not anticipated long silences from Sheryl, as though she was mourning something. Perhaps she was.

"Are you all right, babe?" she asked after Sheryl had cleared the starter plates.

Sheryl heaved a big sigh. "I didn't think it would be so hard."

"Take a deep breath," Kristin said, "you're doing just fine." Depending on their definition of *fine*, this could very well have been a lie, but if it was, it was a white one at most.

"I think you're right about one thing, at least," Sheryl whispered. "I'm going to need some outside help dealing with this."

"Then that's what you shall have." Kristin walked over

to her and took Sheryl in her arms.

"What the hell have I let myself become?" Sheryl's breath was moist in Kristin's ear.

"Nothing a smart and gracious woman like yourself can't come back from." Kristin held her a little tighter.

"Perhaps now would be a good time to tell them a bit more about my decision."

Kristin nodded. "The mains will be out in a few minutes. And yes, I can handle it on my own." She kissed Sheryl on the cheek for a long moment, hoping the imprint of her lips on the soft flesh there could somehow inject her with the power to make it through this more easily.

Then Kristin's mobile phone started ringing. They both jumped, the way they'd been doing every time Kristin got a call since returning from Trevor's, and both of them seeing with their very own eyes the sorry state he was in.

Kristin picked up.

"Is this Sheryl? Trevor Johnson's daughter?" an unknown voice blared through the receiver.

"Yes," Kristin said, because it didn't matter who got the news, and she figured that, either way, Sheryl would be better off hearing it from her.

"This is Harold Robinson from Robinson Funeral Home speaking. I'm very sorry to be the bearer of bad news, but I'm afraid Trevor's no longer with us. He didn't wake up from his afternoon nap. The paramedics have come and gone and he's now in our care. Everything's been taken care of, so no need to worry about practical arrangements."

Kristin found Sheryl's eyes and gave her a small nod. "Thank you for letting me know."

"My condolences, Mrs Johnson," he said, in a tone so practiced it made Kristin's stomach turn. "My thoughts are with you in this difficult time."

Kristin hung up and opened her arms. "It's Trevor," she said. "He's gone."

Sheryl's first thought upon hearing the news was that she needed a drink. To cope with the death of a man who had drunk himself to death, she needed a little something to process it.

"Everything okay in here?" Martha stood in the doorframe.

Sheryl loosened her limp body from Kristin's embrace. "My father died," she said.

"I'm so sorry." Martha stepped closer and rubbed Sheryl's back. "What can we do?"

Sheryl shook her head. "Nothing."

"Shall I whisk Micky and Robin discreetly out of here?" She looked at both of them.

Sheryl figured she didn't reply fast enough, because Kristin said, "Yes, that would be a good idea. Thanks, Martha."

"Consider it done." She squeezed Sheryl's shoulder. "Call me if you need anything at all."

Sheryl watched her walk off, then heard murmurs in the living room. "I should probably say something to them."

"No, babe. It's okay. Stay here with me."

Sheryl did, because she didn't know how she would feel accepting condolences for the death of her father from people who had no idea what her relationship to him was.

After the whispers and shuffles in the living room had died down, Kristin escorted Sheryl to the sofa.

Sheryl's voice came out all shaky when she tried to speak. "I promise you on everything I hold dear that I will stop tomorrow, but will you please pour me a drink?"

Kristin looked her in the eye. "We don't have anything."

"Then let's go somewhere where they do." They lived in Darlinghurst and it was Saturday evening, barely past eight in the evening. There was a bottle shop on the same block as The Pink Bean. Alcohol was everywhere, ready to fill that gaping wound that had just opened in Sheryl's soul.

"I'm not sure that's a good idea." Kristin took her

hands in hers. "Let's talk."

"It's as if he was just hanging on until he had seen me again," Sheryl whispered, changing tack. If Kristin wanted to talk first, fine. She would get that drink later.

"Maybe he was." Kristin stroked Sheryl's palm with her thumb. "The funeral director told me everything was taken care of. That we shouldn't worry about anything."

"How is that even possible?" Sheryl asked. "The man had nothing left."

"The truth is, we don't know what he had and how he arranged for this. He was sober for five months and deadly ill. He could have made all sorts of provisions."

"I don't even know how he got by all those years. I always assumed he was on welfare or something, sponging off the state. He never asked me for anything."

"How could he have?" Kristin tipped her head. "The most important thing is that you don't have to worry about any of it."

"Just show up at the funeral and say my good-byes?"

"If you want to. We don't have to go."

"You know he tried to stop me from going to Mom's funeral. Well, it wasn't an actual funeral, more like a memorial service. Because she had committed suicide she couldn't have a service in the church. Anyway, I insisted on going, sat through the whole thing as stoically as I'd ever been, braved all the glances of those who automatically believed she was a coward for taking her own life. It was horrible, but I had to do it. I was twelve, so not exactly a child anymore. Not someone you can still hide the truth from." Sheryl's voice broke. She coughed, trying to sound like herself again—her old self, no matter who that was or if she would ever be that woman again.

"How do you feel?" Kristin asked.

"I'm not sure. I suppose I'm glad I got to see him before he died. I wouldn't have put it past him to have lied about the state of his health to garner my sympathy, but I guess he was telling the truth." She stared at her hands. "It's just so strange to have any feelings at all about a man who hasn't been in my life for such a long time. But I do feel sad, for him. For the life he could have had. For the relationship we could have had. Mom's death could have brought us closer together, but instead it did the opposite. Perhaps I should have tried more, like you are trying with me now, to get him off the booze. Book him into rehab. Whatever it took. But just like he never had it in him to be there for me, I didn't have that in me either."

"Babe, you should never forget that he was your father, your only remaining parent when you were only twelve. You can't compare the two. You didn't owe him anything."

"At this stage, I think I might need AA *and* a damn good therapist." Sheryl managed a little chuckle, tried to lighten the mood a bit.

Kristin nodded and gave her hands a squeeze.

"When all my friends first started drinking, my wish to not be like Trevor was so great, it easily stopped me from drinking with them. It was just so ingrained in me. It was the most sacred vow I made to myself after it became clear he was destroying himself with booze. It was a given, you know? And I had an answer for every wisecracking boy with a can of cheap beer in his hands who dared to question me. I was so tough back then. I wish I could get some of that back."

"So much happened to you. You carried it all with you in silence for so many years. No child is supposed to go through what you went through. You are so incredibly strong. I've believed that about you ever since you took me to your family's cabin. You are, by far, the strongest person I know. The one who has endured the most. That's how I know you can do this."

"You think too much of me." Sheryl smiled regardless of what she had just said.

"On the contrary," Kristin said, pulled Sheryl toward

her and held her in her arms for a long time.

CHAPTER THIRTY

Sheryl took a deep breath and entered the community hall. Kristin was close on her heels, followed by Martha, Micky, Robin, and Caitlin. It was a Saturday afternoon, two weeks since her father had died, and the room was filled with more people than usual. Sheryl would know, as she'd been there almost every day since she'd started coming ten days earlier.

She hadn't sneaked out for a drink on the day she found out about her father after Kristin had nodded off. Their apartment had remained an alcohol-free zone. On Sunday, they had researched AA meetings together, of which there were at least a few every day spread out over Sydney. Sheryl had chosen a local meeting in Darlinghurst, mostly out of pure convenience. She didn't know any university staff who lived in her area, and if she were to run into someone from school at one of the meetings, she hoped it would become their secret.

Her sponsor, Bert, a man who reminded her of her father, mainly because of his age and spindly frame, greeted her. He had brought his wife and introductions were made all around. Though the crowd was bigger than usual, the atmosphere remained the same: solemn and full of hope.

A very different vibe than when they'd attended Trevor's funeral the week before, where all of ten people had showed up. The mood, as they stood around his grave, had been one of doom and gloom because of the wasted opportunity the funeral of a man who had drunk himself to death represented. If Sheryl were to guess, she figured that she'd finalized her decision, truly vowed and swore on the ghost of her mother, to stop drinking altogether right there and then. It was the only way. And yes, it would be hard, and temptation would always be lurking around the corner, but if the options were dying alone the way Trevor had, a broken and disappointed man, or living a long and healthy life alongside Kristin, then it was an easy choice. Theoretically, at least.

That day, she was sixteen days sober, and she already felt like a different person. Not only because starting the day without a hangover made all the difference, but because of her ability to make the decision. It was clear cut. It was definite. And perhaps Sheryl had her father to thank for it. Perhaps, in his final days on this earth, he had, in some way, managed to come through for her. Though it was too late for him to take any comfort in the fact.

The AA group usually formed a circle, but today they all sat auditorium style because it was an open meeting at which participants had been encouraged to bring their loved ones. Sheryl had brought her true family, which consisted of Kristin first and foremost, but also Caitlin, whom she'd known much better twenty years ago, but that didn't matter —some friends are for life. And Micky and Robin, who had only recently come into her life but had become Pink Bean family, and for whom she felt, at times, an almost motherly affection. And finally Martha, who had bravely come out a few years ago, at the age of fifty-two.

Sheryl didn't know yet if she would speak today. It was one thing to open up to a bunch of strangers who shared her addiction, but another entirely to do so in front of their family and, most importantly, her own. Especially without the loosening effects of alcohol. Because that was, of course, the crux of it all: a life without booze. Without the warm glow of comfort sliding down her throat when she drank vodka. Without the knowledge that after a few glasses of wine on a Friday, everything would be all right. Without the carefree way in which she used to clink her glass against her friends', look them in the eye, and feel so emboldened by the most intoxicating combination of all: friendship and alcohol.

In the end, it didn't matter if she said anything or nothing. It mattered that she was here. And that Kristin and their friends were. And that every morning, when she woke up with a clear head, she could add another day to her tally. The Alcoholics Anonymous age-old adage of "One day at a time," which she had often mocked while tipsy, was the only way forward. Most importantly, though, Sheryl knew that she stood a much better chance than Trevor, because unlike him, she hadn't lost it all. She had Kristin by her side.

When the moderator opened the meeting and asked if anyone wanted to start, Sheryl ignored the usual awkwardness of the moment, and this time made brave by a much more powerful source of intoxication than alcohol—friendship *and* love—she raised her hand, walked to the front of the room, faced the stare of a dozen people she didn't know, and quite a few she knew all too well, and said, "Hi, I'm Sheryl and I'm an alcoholic."

"Coffee on the house," Kristin said as they all walked into The Pink Bean. It was near closing time and the place was empty, save for Josephine who was manning the counter.

"How generous of you, boss," Micky said. "To not make your best employee pay." She winked at Kristin.

"I'll have to dock your wages if you keep talking back to management." Kristin headed behind the counter.

Micky's transformation was the first one she'd witnessed, right from the viewpoint she had now. The Pink Bean was where it had all begun. Only a few short months after Micky had first met Robin, Sheryl's father had walked in. A moment Kristin was sorry she had missed. Perhaps she could have gauged, from the look on Sheryl's face as Trevor made his way to her, what sheer devastation it would cause her, and she would have been more ready for the nightmare it had thrown them into. She wouldn't have let it come this far, but then again, where they were now, headed home after an AA meeting, was probably the only possible outcome for them.

"Caitlin, what can I get you?" Kristin asked.

"I'll have a flat white, please," Caitlin replied.

"The usual for the rest of you, I assume?"

Kristin went about preparing their drinks. A double espresso for Sheryl. A latte—though she would call it a wet cappuccino, for sure—for Robin. Cappuccino for Micky, and a flat white for Martha.

"Josephine, what's going on? You look like you've seen a ghost." Kristin tried to get Josephine's attention. Her stare was glued to Caitlin, and she looked like a deer caught in the headlights.

"Is—is that C—Caitlin James?" she stuttered.

"Yes, it is," Kristin answered. "She's an old friend of Sheryl's. Do you know her?"

"I wish," Josephine sighed. "I've read everything she's ever written, I think. She's the reason I went into Gender Studies."

"Come on over then, I'll introduce you. I'm sure she'll be delighted to meet you."

"I'll just clean up the machine first," Josephine replied, looking quite flustered. "I'll be over in a bit."

Kristin carried the drinks over to the table and then flipped the sign on the door to *Closed* so they had the place to themselves. She glanced over at her group of friends and a warm, fuzzy feeling shot through her at the sight of them in *her* coffee shop. Because, sure, coffee had a ridiculous profit margin, but this place had never been all about the money. It had always, much more, been about the possibilities it offered. A new beginning for her and Sheryl. A sense of community in their new neighborhood. Times like these with friends.

No matter the time they had wasted, this was where

they had ended up. This was how the ebb and flow of life went and The Pink Bean was where they had washed ashore.

———

"What a day." Sheryl sank onto the couch and dragged Kristin with her.

"I'm so proud of you." Kristin maneuvered herself on top of Sheryl's lap, straddling her.

Sheryl looked into Kristin's serene face. Even though she was three years younger than her, she felt twenty years older—at least. Kristin looked so unblemished, her skin so smooth, her eyes so bright.

"And I'm damn lucky to have you," she said, staring up at Kristin.

"If we're going to get all mushy." Kristin leaned in and kissed her softly on the nose, then hard on the lips, stating her intentions.

Sheryl pulled her close. The day had left her exhausted, and the two double espressos she'd had downstairs earlier hadn't helped. Some states of pure emotional fatigue are so deep, even caffeine can't help.

Kristin was already pushing her sideways down onto the couch, not wasting any time.

Just to catch her breath, Sheryl said, "Was there something going on with Josephine? She barely said hello and good-bye before running off home."

Undaunted, Kristin slipped a knee between Sheryl's legs. "She was a bit starstruck by Caitlin, I think. But I would rather not talk about Josephine right now. My lips have better things to do."

Sheryl had no recourse for that. While Kristin trailed kisses down her neck, she let their own history flash through her mind. That very first phone call of which, if Sheryl was honest, she didn't remember much. It was too long ago. She would never forget Kristin daintily jumping out of the cabin of the delivery van, however, in her tight skirt suit and high heels. If she had known then that the woman walking toward her, hand outstretched, would be kissing her like this right now, after all they had been through, she would have taken a second to savor the moment. But that was the thing with life. You never knew who would come and go. Who you would fall in love with and stay with forever—or not.

Here they were, nearly twenty years later—they would need to have a big party next year to celebrate their two decades together—with an entire new history they'd created together between them. From looking at a person the very first time and not knowing a thing about them, to becoming the equivalent of spouses. Perhaps the Australian government would stop being utterly ridiculous by the time they celebrated their twenty years together, and they could actually, legally, get married soon.

Sheryl didn't know what tomorrow would bring. All she knew in that moment, as Kristin's lips reached the hollow of her neck, was that love had seen them through the worst of it. And what could possibly ever stop them after all of that? Sheryl sank deeper onto the couch cushions, Kristin pressing her down with her body weight and her kisses. Sheryl might have lost a lot of love when she was twelve, but Kristin had given her more than she could ever have hoped for since she was twenty-eight. Despite having to join AA, Sheryl knew her dark years had been over a long time ago. And even more lightness had shone upon her on that day she met Kristin.

With one practiced move, she pushed Kristin up a little —she was so slight, it was easy—and slipped out from under her. She toppled Kristin onto her back and stared into her dark eyes.

"This is how we do this," she said.

Kristin smiled up at her. "I know."

ACKNOWLEDGEMENTS

Writing the second book in a series is always difficult for me. This one was no different. After binning a first draft that was 3/4 finished, I decided to write Sheryl and Kristin's story instead of the one I'd previously been slaving over to no avail. It was a relief to plunge into the lives of the Pink Bean owners, but I would be lying if I said writing this book was a breeze. By my standards, it took forever to finish and I had some serious writerly soul searching to do. As always, what kept me going was the unwavering enthusiasm of my wife, who always believes in me no matter how burned out I feel (or how crappy I think my writing is.) I've come to think of this kind of support as normal, but at times it does strike me how rare it is to have found a person who I can always count on, no matter what drama--made-up or real--I've conjured up.

After writing *In the Distance There Is Light*, for a brief period of time, I believed I was done with lesfic. I can now jokingly refer to it as 'The Great Lesbian Romance Burn Out of 2016', but at the time I was less cheerful. In hindsight, I had failed to realise that I'd written myself empty and I needed some time to replenish my writing tank (perhaps the biggest lesson I learned this year.) It, then, came as a huge relief when Carrie, my trusted beta reader, told me she enjoyed this book, despite it being quite a touch darker than Pink Bean Book One. Thank you, Carrie, for the kind words you always have to offer and the endless optimism you show.

Huge thanks to my editor Jason Bradley for dealing with my comma fetish in an appropriate manner and making this book so much better.

As stated in the dedication, my Launch Team is made up of a lovely bunch of people who always have my back. Be it for some last-minute typo-hunting, leaving me the fastest reviews possible, or just cheering me on when I'm suffering from a writerly malaise. (And for patiently waiting for me to emerge form a social media hiatus.) You are all amazing and I can't thank you enough for what you do for me and my books.

This being the last book I'm releasing this year, I feel I should quickly reflect on the craziness of 2016. Some of you may know that I set myself the insane challenge of publishing one book every month in the past year. Obviously, that didn't happen. Nevertheless, 2016 has been my best and most prolific year yet. It has been nothing short of amazing. Despite burn-outs and un-met challenges, I've come to realise my deep love for lesbian romance. I may need to take a break from time to time, but I will never stop writing tales of ladies falling in love (and getting it on.) I just can't help myself. Once again, I must thank you, Dear Reader, for making this extremely rewarding life possible for me, and for going on a journey with me every time I release a new book. Thank you from the bottom of my heart.

ABOUT THE AUTHOR

Harper Bliss is the author of the novels *The Road to You*, *Far from the World We Know*, *Seasons of Love*, and *At the Water's Edge*, the *High Rise* series, the *French Kissing* serial and several other lesbian erotica and romance titles. She is the co-founder of Ladylit Publishing, an independent press focusing on lesbian fiction. Harper lives on an outlying island in Hong Kong with her wife and, regrettably, zero pets. She enjoys talking about herself and her writing process (but mostly herself) on her weekly YouTube broadcast Bliss & Tell.

Harper loves hearing from readers and if you'd like to drop her a note you can do so via harperbliss@gmail.com

Website: www.harperbliss.com
Facebook: facebook.com/HarperBliss
YouTube: youtube.com/c/HarperBliss

CPSIA information can be obtained
at www.ICGtesting.com
Printed in the USA
LVHW03s1532120718
583537LV00001B/42/P